A Chance Reilly Novel

By

Patrick Lindsay

Prologue

Northern New Mexico Territory, 1859

The attack had come with a silent and unexpected ferocity. A squad of fifteen men from Company D, dispatched from Denver just two days before, was crossing a small tributary of the Cimarron River and had no idea the war party was waiting for them. Sergeant Baker, leading the detachment, took the first arrow through the heart and fell silently into the water, dead on impact. Multiple arrows launched only split seconds later found their targets before the soldiers even realized they were under attack. One or two managed to draw their weapons and fire a harmless shot at the Apaches swarming out of the woods, but the shots had no effect. Now only two of them were left.

George Gibson lay face down under the trees, barely daring to raise his head as he watched the Jicarilla Apache warriors walking their horses through the stream, taking guns and ammunition from the dead soldiers, along with any other personal possessions that caught their eye. Gibson glanced sideways at the only other survivor, another private named Campbell who had transferred into the unit only a few days before. Gibson put his finger to his lips needlessly, urging the other man to remain deathly silent. Campbell only nodded, wondering what kind of a fool he would have to be to utter a sound at this point. The warriors reached the wagon at the tail end of the trail of dead soldiers. Gibson watched as they dragged the strongbox containing the gold shipment from the wagon and threw it out on the ground. They used repeated blows from rocks and their tomahawks to eventually force the strongbox open, spilling some of gold coins on the ground.

Gibson raised his head only fractionally higher to see what they would do with the money. Two or three picked up a few of the coins and walked away with them. A fourth knelt, picked up a coin, and after biting it, shrugged and threw it back on the ground. Most seemed to be mounting up to move on, but a handful of them remained on their feet, walking back and forth and checking the tracks they could find leading out of the stream bed. Gibson felt the perspiration break out on his forehead and pour down his cheeks. His pistol was in his hand, but he knew the one shot he could fire would do him little good. He could only hope that their cover under the trees would be good enough.

He, along with Campbell, had been ordered to ride alongside the wagon and told to protect the gold shipment at all costs. The fact that they had been at the tail end of the procession, together with a small amount of cover provided by the wagon, had allowed them to survive up until now. When the sergeant fell, he'd jumped his horse to the far bank, dismounting and using the horse's tracks to cover his own as he'd dashed to the edge of the woods. Upon reaching the trees, he'd slapped his horse on the rump and gone immediately to the ground, worming his way into the underbrush as quietly and quickly as he could. Campbell had seen him and done likewise. Unable to stop him, Gibson had buried his head in the underbrush and hoped his cover hadn't been blown by the new arrival.

Now the Apaches all seemed to be mounting and moving on. Gibson knew it was a near-miracle they hadn't been seen or tracked to their current hiding spot. They remained motionless for an hour or so after all the warriors had apparently left, then Gibson came silently to his feet and motioned for Campbell to do the same. They moved slowly to the edge of the woods and surveyed the scene of the slaughter. Fighting the overwhelming urge to vomit as the buzzards found the carcasses, they looked for any horses that might have returned. They found none. As they turned and began to move back into the tree line, Gibson, acting on impulse, returned to the strongbox and scooped the coins that had fallen out back into the box. He picked up the handle on one side and told Campbell to do the same. They hauled it between them as they left the river bank.

Now they were huddled around a small fire built several feet back from the mouth of a cave. The fire was a danger, but they had to have the warmth as darkness set in. They could only hope that the light wouldn't be visible to any Apaches still in the area. The smoke seemed to diffuse quickly through the trees, and it was too dark to be visible anyway. The pungent smell of the smoke might be a different matter, but Gibson could only hope that the light breeze coming off the mountain would disperse it quickly enough.

He wasn't really sure how far they had walked to get here. They had held to the edge of the tree line as they'd followed the tributary back up in the direction from which they'd come. He knew they couldn't afford to get lost, and it seemed foolish to continue in the direction they'd been going when attacked. They had gone maybe two or three miles, he thought, before he'd seen a tree that could serve as a landmark at the mouth of a faint trail leading back toward the cliffs. They had followed the trail, staying under cover of the trees at the side of it, for maybe a few more miles before reaching the cliffs. Exhausted, cold and hungry, they hadn't hesitated once they had seen the mouth of a small cave. Dragging in whatever dry branches they could find, they had waited for darkness before building a small fire. Now they had some warmth and had gotten a little rest. The hunger wasn't something they could do anything about tonight. Although they had agreed to take turns on watch, the fatigue proved too much and they both fell asleep on the floor of the cave.

Arising at dawn, Gibson grabbed a sharp stick from the pile they had made near the fire and followed his ears to the sound of running water he'd heard from the cave in the early morning silence. As he'd hoped, there were a number of brook trout making their way through the cold rushing water. He waded in, then stood as still as possible with the stick poised over his shoulder. After a number of fruitless tries with the stick, he managed to stab a trout as it swam past. He tossed the fish onto the bank and resumed his efforts, feeling the numbness creeping into his feet already. When he had stabbed a second trout in the near-freezing water, he climbed out and carried both fish back to the cave. He cooked them over the fire quickly, knowing they needed to put out the flame, but also knowing this might be their best chance for food for quite some time.

After eating and extinguishing the fire, the two of them stood near the mouth of the cave, gazing uncertainly at the strongbox full of gold coins. Their original orders had been to transport a private shipment of gold to Fort Stanton, south of here in New Mexico, but that was impossible now. Gibson walked back farther into the cave, able to see more in the early morning light than they had been able to see the previous evening. He stopped when he came to a pile of rocks under a small cave-in area toward the back of the cave. He went back and picked up a side of the strongbox, motioning for Campbell to do the same. They carried it back and buried it under the pile of rocks. Gibson picked up one of the rocks and carried it to the entrance of the cave. Working quickly, he used the rock to scrape a symbol resembling a half moon on the cliff wall to the right of the entrance.

Gibson tossed the rock aside as he began scrambling down the cliff wall outside the cave, slipping in a few spots before he reached the trail below. Campbell followed suit wordlessly. When they were both on the trail, they retreated to the edge of the woods as they had the night before, turned and began walking. The odds of reaching Fort Stanton were near-impossible, but they had no choice. Maybe they could find a horse.

Chapter One

A New Home

Cimarron, New Mexico, 1879

I sat on the porch of my new home and let the fragrant breeze off the mountains wash over me. The late spring was my favorite time of the year. There was still enough chill in the air to occasion the light jacket I had slung over my shoulders, but with the rising sun came the pleasant warmth of the day. I'd done a fair amount of work already that morning, and had stopped only for a quick cup of coffee.

My name is Chance Reilly, and when I say this is my new home, that's only partly true. The land I now own and the house I'm now fixing up belonged to my family when I was a child. I came west with my parents, who were Irish immigrants to this country. They had seen the value of land and were thrilled to have a fresh start, limited only by their ability to take a risk and put in hard work. We had come west over the Santa Fe trail when I was a small boy. I could faintly remember the smell of the prairie grasses and jolting motion of the wagon as we slowly covered ground toward our new home.

Disaster had struck when we were just a few hundred miles from our destination in Cimarron, New Mexico. I'd seen less and less of Mom every day, as she kept to herself in the back of the wagon. I'd had to step up and help spell Dad driving the wagon when he went ahead to scout and sometimes looked in on Mom in the back. One day she didn't come out, and Dad had left me with another family, telling me to wait while they went out and buried Mom.

A snort from the corral roused me from my memories. I walked over the stroked the neck of my sorrel, Archie. We'd been through a few things together. He'd been my first purchase when I'd returned to this area, just a little over a year ago now. I'd had my doubts back then, about whether a man could come home and make good on a new start. But it had all turned out so well for me, after years of struggle and learning that a man had to make his own way and face the things that life throws at him.

I walked around to the back of the house and picked up the hammer where I'd left it before my coffee break. I'd torn down the old boards that had begun to rot and fall away from the house. There was a solid line now of new planks, sealing off the back of the house and protecting it from the cold winter winds that could blow down off these mountains. As I worked, I reflected on how I'd help my dad build this house, many years ago after the wagon train had arrived in Cimarron.

We had carried on after Mom was gone. Dad was determined to build a home and a life for us in the western lands. He taught me how to work with my hands and take pride in what I did. He'd always told me that any man who will work hard and keep trying had a chance for a good life in this country. It's where I got my name. We'd built the house and a small bunkhouse and corral on this property, then put together a small herd on the prettiest piece of land I've ever seen. Just when everything had seemed to be looking up, I'd learned that life can deal some harsh blows, even to the young.

The sound of hoofbeats on the trail out front brought me out from behind the house in a hurry. The best part of my new life was coming to see me, unless I missed my guess. My neighbor and the lady I planned to make a great future with brought lunch every day and stayed to help work on the house for a couple of hours afterward, as she was able. Her father, Jim, was still recuperating from the little range war we'd had to settle with the Carson brothers a few months back. Luckily, he looked to make a full recovery.

"Kate!" I reached up to swing her down from her horse, getting a kiss for my efforts as she handed me the picnic basket she brought every day. "Chance," she smiled, "this is the best part of my day every day." We climbed the steps to the front porch of the house and settled in a couple chairs I'd hammered together for us to use. I made a mental note to do something about the steps we'd just climbed. A couple of them appeared to be on their last legs. I pointed at the steps to distract her while I reached into the picnic basket for the cookies I knew would be in there.

"Hey! Those are for dessert!" She swatted at me as I made an escape with one of the cookies. I happily accepted the slap on my wrist and wolfed down the cookie. "You really should move those to a different spot in the basket," I told her. "That was pretty easy." She chuckled and began spreading the lunch out on a blanket she laid down on the front porch. I noticed she'd moved the rest of the cookies to a spot behind her, though.

Our talk turned to our plans for the two neighboring ranches. Kate Randolph and her father Jim owned the spread immediately to my west. They had been our neighbors as far back as the time when my father and I had been here, more than fifteen years ago. I'd left as a 13-year-old boy after my father's death, sent to live with an aunt and uncle in New York. I'd returned a little over a year ago to reclaim the family property. The Randolphs and I planned to merge the two ranches together. We actually planned to tear down the barbed wire fence between the upper pastures this afternoon. Kate and I planned to live in my old house after I'd finished rebuilding. Jim could stay with us or spend his time in the Randolph house. Either way was fine with us. I knew I owed Kate a good formal proposal, and I planned to make it just as soon as I could prepare this ranch for us.

We finished the lunch she'd brought, washed down with water fresh from the creek that ran across the adjoining properties. I leaned back against the wall of the house. Kate leaned back against me and we looked over the meadow running down from the house, ending in a stand of juniper trees. It was a view I knew we'd never get tired of. After a while she stirred and looked around at me. "Are you still planning to talk to Sam and Mike at the house tonight?" I nodded. "Yes. If they're agreeable, I need to make a trip soon to get some cattle for the place here. I'd like to get them fattening up on the spring grass." Kate and Jim and I had talked at length about cattle for my new place. I had the money to buy some good stock, and didn't much care for what I'd been able to find locally. A short trip and a drive home with some good breeding stock seemed like the plan, assuming I had a couple hands to help me.

Sam ran the saloon in Cimarron, but he didn't seem to mind leaving it for short periods of time if it suited him. I wasn't sure how old Sam was but in any case, he didn't seem to be mellowing with age. He was as salty as ever, and there's nobody I'd rather have in my corner when times are tough. Mike was his young nephew, who'd also stood side by side with us when we needed him. I was hoping they would come with me and that we could make a good plan that evening.

I promised Kate I would be over shortly to help tear down the fence between properties. She headed out and I went around back to finish nailing up a few boards. I remembered helping my dad nail up these old boards, some fifteen years ago. We had finished the house and corral when the three Carson brothers showed up at the house a couple times, talking to Dad about buying the place. He'd turned them down each time, and it seemed to me that the last exchange was getting pretty testy. Then one day he'd simply not come home. I had gotten the sheriff and searched the northern pasture. We finally spotted his body at the base of the cliff on the far northern edge of the ranch. The sheriff had ruled suicide, but I knew better. The Carsons had been up there and had thrown him to his death. Jack Carson had told me as much right before the gunfight that had ended his life.

There was no bringing back either of my parents. The sadness had faded over the years, and I took comfort in knowing they'd be happy with the life I'd been able to make for myself now. All the Carsons were in the ground now. I'd put two of them there myself, along with a cousin of theirs and Kate had saved my life when she shot the third with my father's old Henry rifle.

I walked over to the corral, rubbed Archie's ears for a couple minutes, then saddled him up and rode west toward the fence we were having torn down. Jim had hired a couple guys down at Sam's saloon yesterday, and they had made good progress in removing the fence. We had decided to leave the posts right where they were. It would have been a lot of work to pull them up, and who knew if we might need them again someday. We simply pulled the wire away and rolled it up to store for later use.

Jim, iron-haired, mid-fifties and kindly in a no-nonsense kind of way, was standing at the border of his land and looking across my new pastures. He grinned. "I got some cows can't wait to get at that grass," he told me. "You bring them on over," I said. Kate smiled and walked over to take my hand as we looked at the new pasture we'd created. Jim had a walking stick he leaned on slightly to help with the bullet he'd taken in his leg at almost this exact spot. Sam and I had carried him to his horse and walked him back to the house. His recovery had been slow, but he told me it was improving daily, and he didn't expect it to slow him down. I'd never expected that it would. We stood for a few minutes, estimating the size of the herd we would put on the new pasture, then headed down to the Randolph house for dinner and plans for that new herd.

The Randolph ranch abutted some rocky terrain to the west and sat at the bottom of a gently sloping pasture. The lower pasture served well in the late spring and fall months. The higher northern pasture afforded some good grazing in the summer. During the winter months the cattle were brought down to some lower altitudes. My ranch would work much the same.

Sam and Mike were waiting on the porch when we arrived. Sam had a toothpick in his mouth as always, took his hat off to Kate and grunted briefly when I greeted him. I could see he was putting on his best company manners. Mike, twenty-one and eager to start work for me on the ranch, grinned and good naturedly absorbed the teasing from Jim about coming only for the dinner and when were we going to get some work out of him? Not so long ago the five of us had held our ground on this same patio and behind log piles near the corral, laying down triangulated fire and keeping invaders off our land. I knew Mike was made of some stern stuff and counted myself lucky he was coming to work for me.

We settled around the kitchen table after dinner. I looked around and got the big question out of the way first. "I need to buy some cattle to stock the ranch" I said. "I'm hoping you Sam, and you Mike, can come with me to buy maybe 80 head and drive them back. I'm not finding enough quality cows for sale around here." I stopped and looked hopefully at Sam. He fished in his pocket for a toothpick and stuck it in his mouth. "Well," he mumbled, glancing at Mike, "I've been training that brother of yours to run the bar sometimes. You think Larry can take care of the bar for a few days?" "Lenny" said Mike. "Whatever. You think he can take care of things?" "Sure. He can do it," responded Mike. "Count me in, Chance." All eyes rested on Sam. "Yeah, OK" he said finally. "Long as we're not goin' too far. How far we goin'?"

I leaned forward and placed both elbows on the table. "That's my exact question. Where is the best place to buy some cattle?" I glanced toward Jim and Sam. "I'm hoping you two can offer me some advice on that one. Maybe south of here, somewhere in the territory?" Jim and Sam glanced doubtfully at each other, then Sam finally shook his head. "From what I hear," he offered, "they can play a little rough in that prime grazing area south of Albuquerque. There are some big businessmen and cattle owners who maybe think they own the law. It might come out okay or it might not. My advice would be to steer clear of there. Lincoln county and the areas around there. We don't need the trouble."

That was news to me, but then, I hadn't been around here that long. I glanced at Jim in some surprise. He simply shrugged. "It's the shortest distance to go," I pointed out. I looked back at Sam. "There's no sheriff or lawman to help out if we need him?" I asked. Sam looked up, then back down at the table. "Where law isn't well established, sometimes people can hire a sheriff or two," he told me. "Let's steer clear of there." I decided to drop the idea.

"OK," I said, "where's the next best place? Kansas?" Both Sam and Jim nodded. "Plenty of good cattle in Kansas," Jim said. "Not too far from this part of the territory. You could cover it on the way out in maybe ten days if we keep moving. Coming back with a herd, maybe three weeks or so if you don't push 'em too hard." "Dodge City?" I objected. "Those cattle are pretty worn down when they get there. Besides, I don't want Texas. Those are just trail cattle." Jim agreed. "The native cattle are mostly longhorns, but we can probably find some mixed breeds that would work better for you. Besides, there's some concerns about Texas cattle fever in the ones who've come over the trail. They've kept moving a quarantine line to the west to keep that out of the local herds. You can go a little east of Dodge City to find something. I can keep a couple bull calves and let you have those."

I digested that one for a moment. "OK, that seems right," I said. What's east of Dodge City?" Jim glanced over at Sam, who chewed his toothpick and thought for a moment. "Ellsworth," he said finally. "East of Dodge City, not too far. Of course, you'd want to find a ranch or two in the area willing to sell some cows." He knitted his brows in thought for a moment. "There've been a couple Kansas guys in the saloon a time or two this week. If they show up again in the next few days, I'll see if I can get a name for you. How many did you say you want?"

"Eighty head or so," I told him. "Whaddya think Jim, maybe $25 or $30 a head?" Jim reflected on that one, then nodded. "I don't know a lot about Kansas prices, but that might be the general area. Can you foot the bill?" I nodded and leaned back. "I can." I glanced over at Mike. "You're quiet." Mike grinned. "Not my call," he said. "Besides, I'm not the, expert. I'm ready to work. You make the plan and I'm ready." I looked sideways at Kate. She smiled and patted my knee under the table. "Go get us some cows," she said. "Dad and I can hold the place down for a month."

I pushed my chair back and moved to get up, but Sam held up his hand to stop me. "One thing we don't have," he pointed out. "Besides a wagon for supplies and food, which we can get. We need a cook."

Well, that hadn't occurred to me. "You can't cook?" I asked. Mike rolled his eyes. Sam snorted loudly. "You want us to quit and on day one, you put me to cooking!" he told me. "And don't even look in Mike's direction. The good Lord hasn't made a stomach that can deal with that." I sighed in frustration. Where was I supposed to find a cook? I looked back at Sam. "There must be somebody in town," I said finally. He switched to a new toothpick and chewed it thoughtfully. "OK, maybe," he said at last. "One of the new cafes has a helper that does a bunch of jobs. Washes dishes, serves, fills in cooking sometimes. You could ask. Name's Fred, I think."

"Fred," I grumbled under my breath. "I had a horse named Fred once and I didn't even like him." Kate gave a nudge with her elbow and I changed course. "I'll talk to him. Maybe I can come into town and see if one of your Kansas guys is there. And I'll check with this guy Fred. Everybody good?" There were nods around the table and we stood up and filed out. Sam and Mike mounted and rode out toward Cimarron. Kate walked me over to the corral, gave me a goodnight kiss and went back to the house. I climbed on Archie and headed over to my new house. I rode silently, taking in the night sounds and glancing up at the full moon and stars as I went. I was starting on a new phase of my life and I couldn't have been any happier.

Chapter Two

Planning the Drive

I cantered down the trail toward Cimarron around noon the next day with a number of thoughts on my mind. Details of the cattle purchase and drive were becoming more urgent, but I still felt a strong sense of relief about being able to ride down the trail and into town without running into enemies. Having that part of my life behind me was blissful. I rode Archie up to the rail outside Bart's Saloon which was owned and run by Sam. I don't think he knew who Bart was but apparently he had no interest in changing the name. The same yellow dog lay outside the doors and thumped his tail at me a couple times. I wasn't even sure if I'd ever seen him move.

I pushed on through the doors and waved at Mike behind the bar. He grinned. "Beer?" I looked up at the clock on the wall. Twelve oh five. Well, it had been a thirsty trip in. "Sure," I told him and he set me up. "Is Sam around?" I asked. "Gone down to the mayor's office. Should be back in about five." That's right, Cimarron was getting to be a bigger town now. They had elected themselves a mayor and everything. Dave Purvis owned the general store and now also served as mayor. I leaned my elbows back against the bar and waited for Sam. I surveyed the saloon and saw only one other customer, nursing a beer at a table by himself. Sam came through the doors about five minutes later, just as Mike had predicted.

Sam threw me a wave and joined me at the bar. "Got a couple things for you," he told me. He pointed at the other man in the saloon. "He's one of the guys from Kansas came through here about a week ago. On his way home now. He might be able to help you with buying beef cattle up there. Only name he gave me was Ellis.

Not sure if it's first name or last. Maybe both." Sam grinned to himself. Sometimes his sense of humor needed work. I put down my empty bottle and started toward the gentleman at the table. Another thought hit me and I turned back toward Sam. "You said a couple. What's the other thing?" Sam waved me off. "It'll keep. Talk to him first."

I took a chance it was his last name. "Mr. Ellis?" He looked up. "Just Ellis. You Chance Reilly?" I nodded and sat down. "You have some cattle for sale?" I asked. He shook his head and wiped his mouth with the back of his hand. "No, not me. But I know somebody up there might be willing to sell some. He's a little worried about overgrazing his land." He fished around in his pocket and came up with a pencil, then started looking around for something to write on. Sam noticed and brought over a couple sheets of paper. I motioned for him to join us, so he drew up a chair.

"Man named Lindstrom has a place just a few miles from me," he told me. "On the road between Dodge City and Ellsworth. Well, OK, it's more of a trail than a road." He wrote the name down on one of the sheets of paper. "You want a map?" I nodded. He sketched a route through the northwest part of the New Mexico territory, then on through to Dodge City and Kansas. I noticed it pretty much coincided with the Santa Fe trail, but figured I'd take the map anyway. He pushed the paper to me when he'd finished. I picked it up, asked a few questions about the route, then handed it over to Sam. "Anything else we need to know?" I asked. He thought for a minute, took the last pull from his beer and set the bottle down. "Apaches are a little restless through some of this area." He pointed with the beer bottle at the northwestern part of the New Mexico territory. "I'd keep your head low on the way up there. Coming back, make sure the cattle are rested and ready to go before you reach the border. Then I'd bring 'em on through without stopping. You should be fine when you reach the Canadian river. They'll start to hurry when they smell the water anyway."

I thanked him and put the paper away in my shirt pocket. "What kind of stock will Lindstrom have?" "Mixed breeds," was the answer. "He had a few bulls he brought west with him. Some kind of European breed, mostly. He's been breeding them to the longhorns that have come up the trail. He mostly has short-horned stuff now, and they make better beef cattle than the longhorns. They're still pretty tough and can do a little better than most if you got mountain lions and such."

He stood to go and extended his hand to both of us. I watched him leave, then pulled the map back out and studied it for a minute. It looked like things were coming together. Sam leaned his elbows on the bar. "That other thing I mentioned," he began. I put the map away and gave him my attention. "The mayor – Purvis." I nodded. "He's going to talk to you about being the new sheriff." I immediately began to shake my head and Sam threw up his hands. "I know, I know. I told him you wouldn't be interested, but he's insisting he's going to talk to you about it. Town's still a little unsettled since that dust-up we had with the Carsons a few months ago. At least do him the favor of listening."

After a few minutes of talking back and forth, I agreed to go over and see the mayor. I found him in the general store, stocking a few shelves. He came forward to shake my hand, motioning me to follow him to a couple of chairs at the back of the store. He got straight to the point. "Have you talked to Sam?" I nodded but said nothing else while I waited for him to open the subject. "Sam warned me that you won't be open to this idea, but we do need a sheriff for the town. People are worried about the violence from a few months ago..." He saw the look on my face and held up his hands to forestall what I might say. "I know that you didn't want any of it. As a matter of fact, people really respect the fact that you didn't seek any of it out, but only dealt with what came your way. I ... we here in Cimarron believe you could help keep this town safe."

I waited until he was finished, then explained that I didn't have any desire to be the sheriff – I just wanted to run some cattle on my old family property. He nodded a few times, then asked me about managing the ranch with help while also being the sheriff. When he saw my answer of no was firm, he stood up and thanked me for my time. As I was turning to leave, he made a comment that stayed with me for a while. "Could we," he asked, "still count on you for help if trouble comes?" I turned back and searched his face. "Trouble?" He stared at the floor for a moment, then looked back up. "There are still a few Carson relatives and friends around. A few of us are afraid they'll come looking for trouble."

That was news to me. "I've not heard anything about this," I told him. "What have you heard?" He looked away and seemed reluctant to trouble me with it. "Just a little gossip around town," he said finally. "It may be nothing." I waited a minute longer, but he seemed to have said all he was going to say about it. "If there's that kind of trouble," I told him, "then yes, you can count on me." He seemed relieved, shook my hand again, and showed me out of the general store.

I walked back to the saloon, troubled by what Purvis had told me. I wasn't aware of any more relatives of the Carsons. There'd been that cousin from Mora, but he wasn't around anymore. I had no wish to continue the fight—I hadn't wanted the fight in the first place. I set the thoughts aside as I stepped into the saloon. There wasn't anything else I could do about it right now.

Sam glanced up as I came in, studying my face. "Did you turn him down?" "Yes," I answered, swinging onto a stool in front of the bar. "I've never been a sheriff and have no desire to start now." Sam nodded without commenting further, then leaned his elbows on the bar in front of me. "Well, I've got some good news," he said. "I was over at the café for breakfast this morning and Fred is willing to come on the trip as a cook." "Fred?" I searched my mind and drew a blank. "You, know, we talked about this last night. We need a cook for the trip. Fred is willing." Now the memories came back. I hunched over the stool a little and looked at Sam. I had a bad feeling about this. "Can he cook?" "Yeah," said Sam. "He can cook some beef and beans." I waited to hear the rest, but nothing was forthcoming. "Is that it, beef and beans?" Sam began washing a couple glasses. "He said he made some biscuits one time. You want to meet him?"

"He made some biscuits one time." I stared at Sam, who didn't meet my eyes, but seemed to have a small smirk on his face. "No," I finally said defeatedly. "I guess there aren't many options. He can come." I got up and headed for the doors. I could hear Sam laughing behind me as I pushed through them and began unhitching Archie. That sense of humor needed some serious work.

Before leaving town, I stopped off at the livery stable, where I bought a wagon we could use for the food and supplies, as well as a couple of horses to pull the wagon. I dismounted and waved at the stable owner, Nate, as I came in. He was well known to me from the times when I had kept Archie there. He had an unpleasant surprise for me, as it turns out.

"I need a wagon, fairly good sized one," I started. "Got it!" Nate told me, taking me around to an old wagon in the back. It looked to be in good shape and about the size we'd need, so we haggled for a while and agreed on the price. "Now, just a couple horses to pull it," I told him. Nate shook his head. "You don't need a couple horses; you need a team," he told me. "Unless you plan to spend a fair amount of time teaching them to work together. You got that kind of time?" I didn't have any time. I guess my face told him the story. He took me around to the other side of the stables and pointed out a pair of horses. I guessed they would be slow, but they looked pretty strong. "Here's what you need," he told me. Then he named a price about twice what I'd expected to pay. I tried haggling for a while, but he held firm. I didn't have any options, and it was probably a fair price. Eventually I took the money out of my pocket, paid the $180 he was asking for, and put the meager amount I had left back where it came from. By the time I finished getting provisions and paying for the cows in Kansas, there wouldn't be much of my stake left. "I'll be back for them in a couple days," I said over my shoulder, then headed for home.

Sunup two days later found us gathered outside the livery stable on the north end of Cimarron's main street. I'd said my goodbyes to Kate at the ranch house about a half hour earlier, promising to keep alert and to be safe. It struck me how much I already looked forward to getting back, and how much of a home I now had. It was new to me. I planned to get used to it.

We'd all brought two horses each for the trip. Jim had loaned me a roan horse from his stable to go along with Archie. Sam and Mike travelled light, putting a few extra supplies on their spare horses. Fred would just be driving the wagon. He didn't seem such a bad sort when Sam introduced him. He seemed like he would pull his weight and probably keep to himself a lot. A quick look in the back of the wagon told me not to expect a lot of variety in my diet for the next few weeks. Maybe we could find a good place to eat in Dodge City.

I gathered everybody together for a few minutes to give them the overview of my plans, and to give anybody who had an objection a chance to voice it. I planned to strike out north and east from Cimarron, using the path of the old Santa Fe trail through the Raton Pass and heading directly into Trinidad. From there, the path of the Santa Fe Trail was pretty much the Santa Fe railroad, leading us directly into Dodge City. I figured if we stayed within sight of it, we could keep both from wandering off course and also possibly have a little safety provided by other travelers along the way.

And speaking of safety, I'd given some thought to the possibility of running into a war party here or there. It was the Apaches we would have to keep an eye out for. The Jicarilla tribe was here in the area, along with some Mescaleros. Things were quieter than they had been some years ago, but some promises hadn't been kept concerning a land grant. Hard feelings had followed, as shown by the occasional war party. The government had tried to move them to a reservation near Fort Stanton, south of here, but a great many had refused. The feared names among them, Cochise and Geronimo, weren't something I thought we'd need to worry about. Cochise had died just a few years ago, and Geronimo was known to be operating to the south and west of us. Still, you couldn't be too careful.

Sam and Mike voiced agreement to my plan. Fred just nodded and said nothing, which I had the feeling was going to be the usual for him. The street in Cimarron was still empty with the sun just breaking in the east as we headed out. This would be my life for the next few weeks. I turned my collar up against the cold breeze coming down off the mountains, listening to the creak of the saddle leather and the sound of the horse's hooves. With a little luck, we'd be back in a month with some cattle to start my new ranch.

Kate stepped out on the back porch and threw the morning's dishwater over the rail. She shaded her eyes and watched as her father walked out to the barn to check on a lame mare. She stepped back inside, put on a sheepskin jacket, then pulled her rifle down from a rack near the back door. She had promised to go up and check conditions on the north pasture. It would be warm enough in a few weeks to move their cattle up there for some fresh grazing. The pasture abutted some timber rising up toward the mountains, so she always carried her rifle if she rode near the timberline.

She saddled her horse, tied the rifle onto the saddle, and led her horse out of the corral. As she mounted and rode toward the north pasture, she thought about how much her life had changed in the last year or so. She'd never been unhappy, living on the ranch with her dad, but she admitted to herself she had been lonely before. Her mother had left them when she was young, and Jim never liked to talk about it much. The harshness of western life just didn't agree with some, and maybe that was the case with her mother.

She thought back to the goodbyes she'd said to Chance before he left, standing under a full moon outside the house. A smile touched her lips. Life would never be the same, in the best possible way. Facing challenges and looking at life's possibilities had been enriched in ways she hadn't known. She wanted their lives joined together more than anything. She had, she reflected, killed a man once to save Chance's life.

She urged her horse up the slope and into the pasture, checking the condition as she went. It was greening up nicely. The sound of the stream cutting through the pasture reached her, and she noticed it was much louder than usual. She rode north a little farther and found that the normally quiet stream was extremely full to overflowing. They'd had unusually heavy snowfall that winter, and the melting snow had engorged the Canadian, Cimarron, and other rivers in the area. Clearly the runoff had reached their ranch. She rode along beside the stream for several hundred yards before veering off and completing her circuit of the pasture. All looked good except for the very high level of the stream. That one could be a cause for concern. She reined her horse around and started back for the house.

Reaching the corral, she unsaddled and went to the barn, planning to tell Jim right away about the swollen condition of the stream. She entered and called him a few times, finally realizing that he wasn't in the barn now. A double check of the corral told her he was gone. She shrugged and headed back to the barn. Maybe he'd decided to ride into town to get some supplies. Something in the barn had caught her eye and she went back to see what it was. Rounding the corner, she saw the hay pulled back in the corner of the hay loft, a tarp laying to the side, and an open steamer trunk. Her memories were dim, but she remembered it as her mother's.

She turned around and surveyed the barn and hay loft again. Still no sign of her father, but she knew he must be around somewhere. Finally, curiosity got the better of her and she walked over to the open steamer trunk. She stood over it for a moment, looking at the personal items in the trunk. There were some clothes, a piece or two of jewelry, a hairbrush and a few other things. She knew they had traveled lightly to come west—there probably weren't many other clothes her mother had owned. Kate got down on her knees and began to lift a few things out, looking for any other clues she could find about the mother she had hardly known.

She sifted through a few other odds and ends until she reached the bottom of the trunk. A faded newspaper clipping caught her eye. She lifted it out, smoothing it a bit and noticing how faded and yellow it appeared. She spread it out and read the headline from the Santa Fe newspaper, dated April 17, 1859:

Gold Shipment Remains Unrecovered

$5,000 in Gold Coins Lost After Apache Raid

The sound of approaching footsteps outside told her that her father had returned. She put the clothes back in the steamer trunk and dropped the newspaper clipping on top. Then, on an impulse, she reached down, picked up the clipping, folded it and tucked it into her shirt. She turned to look at her father as he came through the barn door.

Chapter Three

Gibson's Legacy

I could feel the breathing getting a little easier as we came down from the Raton Pass. According to the map I'd been given by Ellis (and I still didn't know if that was a first name or a last name), we were coming down from 7,800 feet at the top of the Raton Pass to around 6,000 feet at Trinidad. I remembered during my gold mining days in the Sangre de Cristo Mountains, I had been able to get accustomed after a while so the thin air didn't bother me, but there'd been no time to make the transition. This was our third day on the road, and everyone was anxious to keep going. Sam and I wanted to get home, Mike wanted to see Dodge City, and nobody knew what Fred wanted.

We'd crossed the Canadian river on the second morning out, and it was deeper than I'd remembered. Sam had commented on the wet winter and the spring thaw. Hopefully it would have dried up a little by the time we came back this way with the cattle. There really wasn't a good alternative to ford the Canadian. Ellis' map had marked a couple spots for a crossing. We'd used one of them yesterday, and I was grateful. We had made camp short of the last climb up Raton, then rolled out early today to get up and over the top. As best I could figure it, Trinidad was only about fifteen miles away now. We could make camp a bit early, then push hard for Dodge City.

I left Mike to follow the wagon, then pulled around to catch Sam, who was taking point and keeping a sharp eye out. He'd had some experience with the Apaches in his younger days and wasn't keen on repeating them. We didn't have the best cover because the aspens were just beginning to leaf out. We tried to keep the noise to a minimum and avoided sky lining ourselves on the ridges. I saw Sam's horse around the corner and gave Archie some gentle pressure to catch up.

Sam topped a rise as I came up to him. He reined in to observe the trail below, then held up a hand to stop me. I waved back at Fred to stop the wagon, then dismounted and came up quietly beside Sam. He removed the bandana from around his neck and stepped forward to muzzle his horse with it, and I did the same. I followed his gaze and saw a small party of Apaches working their way through the juniper trees below us. I counted four of them, but they didn't appear to me to be a war party. They might have been a hunting party, I thought. Taking no chances, we remained still while they filed through below us. When they had passed, we motioned for Mike and Fred to join us, then remained where we were for another hour or so before continuing.

We were well down below the snowline now, pausing sometimes to water our horses in the cold streams of mountain water flowing through the area. I made a mental note to hook up a line for a little trout fishing on the way back. Maybe a break from the delights of Fred's relentless beef and beans menu would be even more welcome by then. Eventually we came within site of Trinidad. We rode into town, found a café for some dinner, then took a couple rooms in a hotel just a couple doors down. I took out my map and made some estimates on the distance left. The difficult part of the journey in terms of terrain and safety was behind us. With a little luck and some early starts, I figured we could be in Dodge City five days from now.

Kate and Jim sat across the kitchen table from each other. Jim shifted uneasily in his chair, meeting her eyes only occasionally. Kate reached out and took his hand. Jim cleared his throat and began uncertainly: "I know I never talked to you much about your mother. You were so young when she left..." His voice trailed off uncertainly. "It's OK Dad. I was a child and I'm sure you didn't know what to tell me. It's been a long time. I'd like to know more about her now, and why she left us. Do you even know why?"

Jim shrugged and cleared his throat a few times before starting again. "We were agreed to come west... at least I thought we were. Times were hard for us in Maryland and it seemed pretty certain that a senseless war was coming. I was afraid we'd be right in the middle of the battles if war came. We packed up when you were little and came out here. I loved it and found a new start here. I guess your mother wasn't as happy." He stared at a spot on the opposite wall for a while. "Did she ever tell you she wasn't happy?"

Kate asked. Jim returned his gaze to his daughter. "No, not in so many words. Maybe there were a few clues I should have picked up on. She talked sometimes about California. San Francisco is what she mentioned the most often. I was so wrapped up in getting this place going I guess I didn't pay enough attention. I thought maybe we could all take a trip out there together sometime." He shifted his glance again. "We were so young then, you know... I was twenty-five and she was only twenty-one when we came here."

Jim sat in silence for a moment, then seemed to gather himself to finish the story he'd started. "One day I was out working the north pasture and I had taken you with me. You were only four, but you loved coming out to see the baby calves. We came home late, just as it was getting dark, and your mother was gone. She had taken maybe only half the clothes she had, and there weren't that many to start with. She left in a hurry and travelled light. There was only a short note, telling me this place just wasn't for her and not to try to follow her. I probably would have followed anyway, but I had you to consider, so I never did. For a long time, I thought she would be back. Sometimes the wind would blow the door a little at night, and I thought it might be her coming in... it never was. I'm not sure what made me look in that trunk again today. It had been a very long time." His voice trailed off again, and Kate felt a momentary regret at stirring the painful memories. She had wanted to ask about one more thing, but maybe this wasn't the time.

She looked up to find her father's eyes on her. "If there's anything else, Kate, just ask me now. I've kept quiet about this for too long already. What is it?" Kate hesitated only a moment before pulling the newspaper article from her shirt and spreading it out on the table. She turned it around so her father could read the title, but he seemed to know it by heart already. He covered his face with his hands and mumbled the word "Gibson." Kate masked her instant curiosity and waited for him to start again.

"Did you read the article?" he asked. Kate nodded. "I read through it quickly one time. It seems to talk about a shipment of gold coins lost in the mountains somewhere near here." "An army payroll or something?" She waited for a moment. "What does this have to do with Mom?" Jim started to answer, fell silent, then finally began to talk again. "So, you've read the basics about the story. There was a company of soldiers ordered to bring a shipment of about $5,000 in gold coins from Denver to Fort Stanton, south of here. The story went around that it was army payroll, but it wasn't. That's too much money for a payroll. It was a private shipment. Somebody had enough money and influence to get army protection. The soldiers were attacked by a war party of Jicarilla Apaches and destroyed. Only two soldiers were left, and they supposedly buried the money near the Raton Pass, maybe one hundred miles from here, intending to come back with more soldiers to recover it. Then they made a run for the fort. One was killed on the way there, leaving only one soldier, a man named George Gibson, with the knowledge of the gold."

Kate leaned forward, fascinated by the story she was hearing for the first time. It struck her immediately that her father was reciting some details about the story not contained in the news article. Not wanting to interrupt, she pressed her father's hand, mentally urging him on. Jim sipped from a glass of water on the table, stared at the opposite wall again for a moment, then continued:

"George Gibson returned to the fort, but never told his officers about burying the gold. He told them the Apaches had taken it and he had no knowledge of its whereabouts. Three weeks later he went AWOL and left Fort Stanton, never to return. The army sent troops to the area and engaged the Apaches in a few running battles, but they never learned about the burial of the treasure." He stopped and looked at Kate over the top of his water glass. "I'm sure you're wondering how I would know anything beyond what is in this article." He picked up the article, folded it once and returned it to Kate. "I know this because George Gibson showed up at our doorstep after he ran away from the army."

Kate was once again floored. How had this all remained a secret for so long, even from her? She leaned back and simply waited for the rest of the story. Jim turned his chair sideways and looked out the window as he continued. "He showed up at our doorway, broke and hungry. He had a small wound, apparently from the fight with the Apaches. He didn't give us his real name at first, in fact, he never gave me his real name. He stayed on here for a couple weeks, doing a little work for me. I guess he came to trust your mother and told her how they had buried the treasure, left it there and made a break for it. His partner was killed before they got very far away, but he made it back to the fort. Gibson claims the owner of the gold died in the attack also. They would have made him a soldier or someone disguised as a soldier. Crazy story all the way around." He paused. "And then he deserted," prompted Kate. Jim turned around to face her again. "Yes, he deserted and wound up here."

"And then left after a couple weeks?" Kate asked. "Yes," her father answered. "He left here after a couple of weeks. Your mother told me what he'd told her about the buried money. Apparently, he was headed back to retrieve it. According to your mom, he told her quite a bit about where it was buried. Your mother left about ten days after that. I never saw her again."

Kate let the silence hang for a while before asking the one additional question she needed an answer to: "Dad, did she... run away with him?" Jim looked up at her, the pain evident in his eyes. "I didn't think so for a long time, maybe just because I didn't want to. There were about ten days that went by between the time he left and the time she left. Maybe she just decided there wasn't enough adventure in her life and left after those stories from Gibson. The thing is, it wasn't safe for a woman travelling alone... not all that safe for a man travelling alone. Would she really have just struck out on her own, headed for San Francisco or who knows where? Doesn't seem likely." Kate nodded and looked down at the table. It seemed odd, discussing her mother and things she had done when she was several years younger than Kate presently was.

Jim paused, clearly deciding whether he should say anything else. Kate sensed this might be the most painful thing of all. "What is it, Dad?" Jim dropped his eyes to the floor and cleared his throat. "The other reason I didn't want to believe she went with him is because of what happened to him." Kate braced herself mentally and waited. "He no doubt went back for the treasure, but it doesn't look like he got there. The Santa Fe paper ran an article a few weeks later, saying that his body had been found near the pass where he told your mom that the gold had been buried. He'd been killed by Apaches." Kate drew in a sharp breath, feeling the tears start down her cheeks for a mother she hadn't really known. "And Mom?" Jim shook his head. There was no mention of it. I did manage to check with a sergeant I knew down at Fort Stanton. There was no body found besides the body of George Gibson. There was no evidence of a woman having been with him at the time of his death."

Kate breathed a small sigh of relief. It left open the question of what had become of her mother, but it would have been unbearable to think of her dying as George Gibson had. Jim got up abruptly and left the house, headed for the corral and barn. She knew he would plunge into work to help himself in not thinking about something he had no doubt agonized over many times. It was his way of dealing with unpleasant things, and she had come to understand it long ago.

She leaned back in her chair and looked through the kitchen window, her fingers idly resting on the newspaper clipping in front of her. If her mother hadn't suffered the same fate as George Gibson, what had become of her? She hadn't asked her father if he had ever heard from her afterwards, but she was sure the answer was no. She believed he would have left no stone unturned to find her if he thought she was alive. There was also the question of the buried gold coins. With George Gibson dead and no sign that her mother was alive, there was no one who even knew it had been buried intact except for her and her father. She wasn't going to ask him any more questions about that now. It didn't seem all that important and she knew it was all a very painful memory for him. She got up and went outside to start on some afternoon chores.

We came within view of Dodge City and the pace quickened. It was something like a herd sensing the end of the trail. And we didn't even have any cattle yet. The herd was just Sam, Mike and Fred and I have to admit I was ready to hit town myself. Mike ranged up alongside of me, and I could see the excitement in his eyes. "Have you been to Dodge City before, Chance? What do you know about it?" "No," I answered. "Never been here. The wagon train passed right by here when I came west with my parents, but Dodge City didn't exist yet. It only started maybe five years ago. It was a good stop-off for buffalo hunters at first, then quarantine laws pushed the cattle herds from Texas farther west. And the railroad came through. I guess all of it together helped build Dodge City. I'll get Sam to tell us a little more before we go out later. We need to be a little bit careful."

We paused as we entered town and Sam looked around. "Guns off here," he said, and Mike and I followed suit by taking off our gun belts. Fred apparently never carried a gun, but he'd kept a Winchester 73 rifle handy when we were travelling. We rode up Front street and pulled in at the Dodge House Hotel. Fred continued on down the street to the livery. We waited while he dropped off the wagon, then went inside and got a couple of rooms. "Let's take a half hour or so then meet back down in the lobby," I told them. "I want us all to leave Dodge City intact tomorrow."

When we reconvened in the lobby, we had left our guns up in the room. "Sam," I said. "Tell everybody what we need to know about Dodge City." Sam stroked his mustache for a minute, then started: "Been a couple years since I've been here," he said, "but here's what I know. Lot of money flowing in this town. First it was the buffalo hunters, coming in here with hundreds of dollars in their pockets from those buffalo hides and dying to spend it. The buffalo ran out a couple of years ago, but the cattle boys, mostly from Texas, took their place. You'll see saloons named 'Lone Star' and 'Alamo'. That's to get those Texas boys to spend their money. Trouble can follow money."

He paused and stuffed his hands in his pockets. I think he was starting to enjoy the captive audience. "There's two halves to the town," he said. "North side and the south side. North side is tame and kept under tight wraps. No guns allowed on the north side. That's why ours are upstairs. The marshal and his deputies don't mess around. South side is a lot wilder. More'n twenty saloons and all kinds of stuff. We'll pretty much keep to the north side so we can leave in as good a shape as we got here. Any questions?" Nobody said anything, but Mike was shifting from one foot to the other and I knew what he was dying to ask.

"Is it about the Long Branch, Mike?" I asked. He nodded vigorously and even Fred seemed to perk up a bit. "We can't come to Dodge City without stopping at the Long Branch," he said emphatically. I chuckled and noticed that even Sam had a little smile on his face. "OK," I relented. "We'll go to the Long Branch after we've had some dinner." I led the way to a café across the street where we had, what else, steak. I had to admit it was pretty tasty. We found our way to the Long Branch Saloon and pushed our way in, finally finding a table. I looked around, seeing every kind of gambling I'd ever heard of going on. Maybe a couple kinds I'd never heard of. I heard some music and stared into the corner. There was a five-piece orchestra playing. "Well I never," began Sam, his voice trailing away. Fred's jaw dropped and I must admit that mine was half-mast. "Never heard of such a thing in a saloon," I finally managed to say.

"Howdy boys. Enjoying your evening?" I looked up to see a badge on the man's chest. "Marshal," I nodded. He extended a hand. "Name's Ed Masterson. What brings you boys to Dodge City?" I explained that we were on our way to buy a herd near Ellsworth. He seemed satisfied, then turned as he was leaving, gesturing behind him. "Meet my deputy, Wyatt Earp." I looked over into one of the coolest, most calculating pair of eyes I'd ever seen. Maybe the coldest eyes I'd ever seen.

Chapter Four

Dodge City

Masterson moved on and Wyatt Earp remained for a moment. His eyes travelled over each of us, checking for guns, and he asked me again about the herd we intended to buy in Ellsworth. He seemed satisfied and nodded, somewhat agreeably. His attention was caught by a poker game in the corner and he moved in that direction. "Anybody know anything about him?" I asked. "Sam?"

Sam slugged down a huge mouthful of beer. "Nope," he said. "Been a couple years since I've been here and he wasn't here then." His eyes followed Earp across the room. "All business, that one," he concluded.

A dance hall girl who apparently doubled as a waitress brought Mike a second whiskey and lingered for a moment, flirting with him. When she moved on, he watched her go, silly grin pasted all over his face. "Mike," I said, "how old are you?" It took him a second to register the question. He tore his gaze away and looked at me, knowing that I knew the answer. "Twenty-one," he said finally, his eyes asking why I'd asked.

I took a sip on my drink and leaned back. "How bad do you want to live to be twenty-two?" I asked. Sam snorted into his beer. Across the room, Mike's serving girl stopped to flirt with another customer, but this one started to get handsy. There was a shout, and a guy came flying out from behind the bar. He tackled the customer. They rolled on the floor and fists started to fly. Masterson and Earp appeared immediately, pushed back the customers who had started to crowd in, grabbed the combatants by the collar and separated them. One of them was escorted back behind the bar and the customer was shown out in a none-too-gentle fashion by Earp.

I watched as things started to settle back down, then observed to nobody in particular: "Yeah, twenty-one is a pretty good age, but twenty-two is pretty good, too." Sam nodded emphatically. Mike, looking a little sheepish, surveyed the room as waiters picked up a couple tables and chairs. "Was that a bouncer or a boyfriend?" he asked no one in particular. "Maybe both," said Sam. Mike digested that information for a second, then asked "Why do you think she does that?" "Hard to say," I answered after a short silence. "Maybe she hasn't figured out how much trouble it can lead to. Maybe she likes watching guys fight over her. Whatever it is, she's bad for your health." There was general agreement on that one. We finished our drinks, listened to the orchestra for a few more minutes, then moved out of the Long Branch without visiting the gaming tables.

We moved on up Front Street toward the Dodge House, watching the street as it teemed with cowboys, no doubt with pockets full of money, headed for the south side of town. I was sure those pockets would be a lot lighter when they came back, but maybe they knew that. We stopped in front of the hotel to watch for a while longer. "How long do you think it can stay this busy around here?" I asked Sam. He shrugged. "The quarantine line keeps moving west. People are establishing more herds out here. The longhorns aren't good beef cattle, just the only game in town for now. I'd guess maybe ten more years." We watched in silence for a while longer. Masterson rode by and tipped his hat when he recognized us. We nodded as he rode by.

Eventually I looked around and started moving up the steps toward the room. "We'll ride out at six in the morning to get up to Ellsworth and get a herd," I told them. "You boys do what you want, just stay in one piece and be ready to go at six."

Kate surveyed the cattle as she rode along the north pasture near the overflowing stream cutting through it. The cattle looked healthy, but she and Jim had decided they needed to be moved back down to the lower pasture on the south side of the ranch. Normally they grazed the cattle on the north pasture starting about this time of year as temperatures climbed, but the widening, rushing stream had them concerned. Spring thaws had brought a great deal more water than they'd seen in some time, and now it had been compounded by several days of hard, driving rain.

She turned her collar up against the rain and rode to the far western edge of the pasture, up against the timber and rocky cliffs that began pushing upward. She looked to the north, where there were scraggly patches of trees and mudholes that ended in rocky faces and shelves climbing up to the mountains. There were rivulets of water running down in many places. Her father had told her he'd be up presently to help drive the cattle. They needed to work to the east to get to the trail leading to the south pasture, so she began to push them slowly to the east.

She thought about Chance as she moved the cattle. By now, he should have reached Ellsworth and was hopefully on the way home with his new herd. She wondered if he would propose when he returned. She'd gotten to know him well in these last few months and she felt sure he was planning on it. He might have bought a ring in Dodge City... a small smile played across her lips. Her thoughts turned to her mother and the smile disappeared. It was disquieting to not know what had become of her. If she'd gone to San Francisco and things hadn't turned out as expected, she would have come home, wouldn't she?

A sound on her left pulled her abruptly from her thoughts. She looked to her left, up toward the mountains, and what she saw horrified her. There was a solid wall of mud and boulders pushing its way down the slope, flowing around the occasional tree in its path and over the rocky ledges. Some of the boulders were bouncing ahead of the wall of mud. At the same time, she heard a voice and looked across the pasture to see Jim waving his hand above his head and shouting frantically, "Kate, GET OUT of there!"

She put her spurs to her horse and he leaped forward, seeming to sense the danger. The roar from the mudslide was building. She hung on grimly, weaving her horse through the cattle as they turned and started to run. As the herd began to stampede, she tried to work her way to the edge of them. She saw her father turn his horse and begin to run to the south, avoiding the stampede. A quick glance to her left showed that the thicker tree line was slowing the slide as she rode away from it. As quickly as it started, she found herself working her way free of the stampeding herd and out of range of the slide. She rode to her father's side, seeing the fear for her still etched on his face. She leaned over in the saddle as he wrapped his arms around her in a hug.

They turned to look back as the mudslide began to slow. Kate guessed that maybe two thirds of the herd had escaped. Some were clearly dead, lying at odd angles, killed by a boulder or maybe stunned and then suffocated in the mud. The rest were still stampeding to the east, but she knew they would calm down and stop before they reached the edge of the ranch. She turned back and started after her father, who pulled out his rope and began to shake out a loop. Some cows were probably impossibly stuck in the mud and too far away to rescue, but there were some at the edge they could possibly pull out.

Jim cast a loop on a cow at the edge of the slide area that didn't seem able to pull out of the mud. He gestured at Kate. "Throw your lasso on her, too. Our horses pulling together have a better chance of getting her out." She cast a loop as well, and the horses pulled the heifer from the mud, bawling. Working in tandem, they located two more cows trapped in the mud but within range of their lassos. They succeeded in pulling both out to solid ground, but Kate knew their horses were tiring, and she didn't see any others close enough to rope. She surveyed the expanse of mud and rock in front of her. Some were down and not moving; a few seemed twisted at odd angles and she knew they may have been struck by a rock or perhaps killed by being bowled over and rolling through the suffocating mud.

Kate looked over at her father, who was looking out at the same scene she was taking in. He shook his head in frustration. "We can't afford to lose a horse out there, or get stuck in it ourselves. Maybe...". He left the thought unfinished. There didn't seem to be anything they could do for the others. Kate estimated they had lost or would lose at least fifteen cows. It was a quarter of their herd or more, and they could ill afford it. She mopped her brow with her bandana and waited for her father to say something more. His shoulders were slumped and he shook his head as he sat his horse at the edge of the slide.

In front of them, maybe fifteen feet away lay a heifer who had clearly been killed in the slide. She lay motionless, head twisted at an odd angle. Kate shifted her eyes away. As she looked across for any others they could possibly rescue, a faint but steady bawling noise reached her ears. She looked over at Jim, who had focused his attention on the far side of the dead heifer. He moved suddenly to shake out a loop, then rode into the mud as far as he dared. He cast the loop, missed, then cast again. As he backed his horse out to safe ground, Kate could see a small calf being pulled out from behind her dead mother.

When his horse had backed out of the mud, Jim wrapped the lariat around his saddle horn and climbed down. The horse held his ground as Jim waded in and picked up the calf. He carried her to a safe place and set her down, checking for injuries. She appeared to be fine. Getting a firm grip with one arm, he removed the lasso, carried the calf over and set her across Kate's saddle. He used Kate's rope to tie her onto the saddle. A small smile creased his face for the first time that morning. "Bottle feeding project for you," he said, returning to his horse. "Nothing else we can do here now," he added, without turning to face her. "Might as well take her down to the barn."

Kate knew that he would stay for quite some time, looking for any other animal he might save, but she also knew that it was true there was nothing further either one of them could do. She turned for home, riding easily and occasionally patting the calf to reassure her. She reached the corral about fifteen minutes later, taking the calf down and locking her in the barn before returning to unsaddle her horse. When she returned to the barn, it took her another ten minutes to find the bottle she had used the last time she had hand fed a calf. She tried to remember how long that had been.

She found some milk that had been stored in a cool corner of the barn that morning and filled the bottle. Sitting down on a stool she normally used for milking, she coaxed the hungry calf over for the first of many bottle feedings. She estimated the calf was less than a week old, smiling as she remembered how strong a pull came from such a small animal when food was involved. When they were finished, she washed the bottle and sat down on the back porch of the house, thinking about the losses they'd had that day. It wasn't a total disaster, but it was a blow nonetheless.

Her thoughts returned to Chance as she considered the extremely high levels of the creeks and rivers. The rain had been relentless for several days now. Chance and the others would be bringing a herd through from Kansas. The first part of the return trip probably wouldn't be too bad, but there was no avoiding some high waters and possible flooding on the creeks and rivers when they reached the northeastern New Mexico territory. She knew he would be careful but she wished there were some way to send a message to him. The exact route hadn't been planned. They had made a couple of options, designed to give them flexibility to deal with possible Indian problems or weather-related trouble. She could think of no reliable way to reach him. She looked up to see Jim walking his horse into the corral, and resolved not to worry about things she couldn't control, she walked out to see if there was anything yet to be done to salvage the herd.

The return trip had been uneventful so far, but then this was the uneventful leg of the trip. We pretty much stayed within sight of the Santa Fe railroad and occasionally met up with a few other horseback travelers. I'd been able to buy what I'd hoped for in Ellsworth. Lindstrom hadn't been much of a talker—I wasn't too sure I'd gotten more than thirty or forty words out of him, but then again, I was there to buy cows, not talk. He'd had a herd of longhorns mixed with some other breeds that might make decent beef cattle. I'd bought mostly heifers, about sixty-five head. I'd also picked up about a dozen young steers that I thought I could fatten up over the next year or so and sell for the meat. It could give me a little cash faster than raising them from calves. I hadn't really liked the bulls he had, so I didn't buy any. Jim had three that were better than any of Lindstrom's I'd seen, and he'd lend them to the extent they could serve my cows as well as his. Maybe I would still be able to buy a couple closer to home that suited me a little better, as long as they didn't cost too much. Between buying the ranch back and fixing up the house, along with these cows, I'd just about spent the money from mining in the Sangre de Cristo Mountains last summer.

We'd been on the trip for almost a month now, and at times I found myself dozing in the saddle from the sheer repetition of the drive, day after day. We'd settled into a routine. I took the point, with Sam on the left flank and Mike on the right. Fred brought up the rear in the wagon, though we all switched out at times to give him a break from the dust kicked up by the herd. We had a point steer, mostly longhorn, that seemed to make a good leader for the bunch. I had a feeling there had been a drive up from Texas not too far in his past. I'd named him Horns for lack of any original ideas. I'd taken him at Lindstrom's recommendation, and there hadn't been a day on the drive I hadn't been glad I had him.

As the plains of western Kansas gave way to the southeastern corner of Colorado, we all picked up the pace a little. I'm sure each of us had his own reasons for wanting to get home. I couldn't wait to get back and see Kate. Sam was a little antsy at having left the saloon in the care of his younger nephew. Mike was looking forward to moving out and working for us full time at the two ranches. I'm sure Fred had his reasons too, but he pretty much kept them to himself.

The monotony began to give way as we climbed toward Trinidad. The end of the Santa Fe railroad was there, though I knew there were plans and some construction under way to push the railroad on through into the New Mexico territory. I wondered in passing if Kate might enjoy a trip to Dodge City when the rail lines were complete. The plans I'd heard of had them passing near us. I called a halt before we came to Trinidad and let them graze while I talked to the crew. We obviously had a different situation than we'd had on the way out as we were coming back with a herd. We were all mindful of the advice we'd received to rest the herd somewhere around here, then push them as quickly as we could over the Raton pass and through the Jicarilla Apache territory. We decided to drive them a few miles past Trinidad, stop where there was water, and rest them for a day before the final push.

Three days later found us well down the other side of the pass and headed for home. We'd left at daybreak the morning after resting the cattle, stopping before we reached the snow on the pass, then driving over and down. We'd known there was snow on the pass from our trip out, but the herd came through it in good shape and our spirits were lifting as we got closer. One thing was nagging at me, though, and I found myself increasingly troubled. We'd had good luck all the way, but the streams we were crossing were running very high. The snowmelt had no doubt caused a lot of it, but by the looks of things there had also been a great deal of rain since we left.

I glanced back to my left, dropped back a little bit and let Horns push forward, then motioned Sam to come up a bit and join me. He rode up, rolling the ever-present toothpick in his mouth and glancing back at the stream we'd just crossed. He pulled up and glanced at me quizzically. "Is it my imagination," I asked, "or are these streams we're crossing really swollen now?" Sam shook his head. "Not your imagination," he said emphatically. "I'm gettin' a little worried about it too. Wonderin' what the Canadian river looks like right now." I absorbed that one for a while, then asked the obvious question. "If we don't ford the Canadian again to get home, do we have a better way of getting there?" Sam again shook his head. "I don't think so. This ain't the safest country to lollygag around it, what with Apaches and all. It would cost us a lot of time and backtracking to do something else."

We rode along in silence for a while. I turned it over in my head every way I could think of, and finally came to the same conclusion. "OK," I said. "I can't see any other way either. We'll be to the river before too long. Maybe it won't be too bad."

About two hours later I heard the roar of rushing water. The Canadian was clearly running high. I wondered how high it was and if we could cross it after all.

Chapter Five

The Force of Nature

We gathered at the place where we'd forded on the way up. At least, we were pretty sure it was where we had forded the Canadian before. The noise had built to a gentle roar, the water rushing past us, nearing overflow on both sides. Branches and leaves bobbed on the surface, rushing around the occasional rock showing above the frothing surface of the river. We studied it in silence, nobody voicing his thoughts for the moment. The herd had spread out along the edge to water, apparently not afraid of it, but not showing any big urge to cross it either.

I polled the group on what they wanted to do. Nobody wanted to backtrack through Apache country, and none of us felt optimistic about finding a better place to cross. Probably uppermost on our minds was the idea that time was crucial here. The runoff from the mountains was only increasing as the weather warmed, and the skies looked threatening right now. Any more volume of water in that river was a huge problem. Fred voiced doubts we could cross with the wagon, and it seemed pretty obvious he was right. That bulky wagon, pulled by one horse, could never make it. We voted immediately to unhitch the wagon and leave it there. Maybe I'd be back some day to get it, or maybe we had just donated it to whoever came through when water levels were down. They could have the beef and beans left in the back. I was prepared to live on roots and berries the rest of the way anyway.

We unhitched the wagon and left it on the eastern bank of the river. I rode Archie into the river for a short way. His ears came back a bit, but he seemed willing to swim it. I turned him back and we began to bunch the cattle for the crossing. Horns had apparently seen some high water before—he wasn't pulling back from it. We decided to make the crossing with me on the point, Fred on the left flank and Mike on the right. Sam volunteered to bring up the rear and urge the slower ones across. It was the most dangerous position, but Sam was insistent, and probably better able to do it than any of us. I led the way in. Archie hesitated, then began to swim, with Horns following him in. We were pushed around a little and I felt the strength of the current against my leg, but Archie swam steadily. Glancing around, the herd was more spread out than I would have liked, but Fred had entered on my right, his horse swimming steadily on the far side of the herd. Mike had done the same on my left, though he was too far downstream for my comfort. Sam was urging the stragglers into the water on the eastern bank.

After several minutes spent with Archie swimming steadily across, I realized we were farther downstream than where we'd started, but it was a wide fording area and we still had room on the far side. I sensed the water growing shallower, and as Archie began to find footing on the western bank, I glanced back one more time. Fred and Mike were holding the flanks and making good progress. Sam had urged the last stragglers into the water and he had also entered the river. I breathed a little easier and began to feel a little relief creeping in. Archie had begun to splash up on the shore when the volume of noise on my right shot way up. I looked that way and saw a solid wall of water rushing toward me. The thought flashed through my mind as I screamed a warning to the others: *"Flash flood!"*

Time seemed to slow down by half. I turned, feeling like I was moving in quicksand. There was nothing I could do suddenly enough. My brain registered shouts from Sam and Mike as they tried to move the cattle through. At almost the same time, I saw the wall of water crash into Fred on the flank, sweeping him off his horse. I tried to urge Archie forward to help, but he wasn't budging, which probably made him smarter than me. I saw Sam leaning out of the saddle, grabbing Fred by the collar as he was swept by. I heard cattle bawling as they were knocked off their feet and swept down the river, some turning over and over as they went. On the far flank I saw that Mike had gotten through far enough to climb out on the western bank. Horns and several more cattle seemed to have made it through.

It was Sam and Fred I had to worry about now. I could hear Mike spluttering on the bank as he crawled out of the river. His horse scrambled off into the woods. Sam was still hanging onto Fred somehow, but Fred didn't seem to be moving and Sam and his horse were being swept rapidly downstream, cattle bawling and flailing all around them. It was a miracle Sam was still on his horse and holding on. I turned Archie and raced downstream along the bank, shaking out a loop. I splashed into the edge of the river and flung the rope as hard as I could, screaming for Sam to grab the rope even as another surge from the river threatened to drown out my words. I don't know if Sam heard me over the roar of the water or just saw the lasso splash down, but he grabbed it and slung it over his shoulders even as the flood tore Fred from his grip.

I stopped Archie on the bank of the river and began backing him up. A quick look behind told me I had twenty feet or so to work with before we'd be stopped by the trees. Sam had his head up and he settled the rope around him, holding on with both hands now. From the corner of my eye I could see Fred being swept away around a bend, and he appeared to be face down. We backed Sam slowly through the river. He took a glancing blow from a steer as it tumbled past him, but his head was still up and he had one hand on the rope. The other appeared to be holding his side now. Archie continued to back up, and from the corner of my eye I saw Mike in a stumbling run toward us. He grabbed the rope, set his feet and began to pull. When Archie reached the tree line I leaped off, grabbed the rope and pulled along with Mike.

When Sam reached shallow water, he appeared to be trying to crawl out, but he wasn't making much progress. I wrapped the slack rope around the saddle horn and raced forward, reaching Sam at the same time Mike got there. We pulled him from the water and laid him out on the bank. He was moaning, spluttering, and spitting up some water, but he was alive. I collapsed on the bank in relief. Mike was staring down the river where Fred had disappeared, then turned around to look at me. I shook my head. Mike heaved a sigh and sat down heavily. Sam was clutching his side and groaning loudly. We carried him as gently as we could to a safer spot, higher up on the bank, and made him as comfortable as possible.

We all lay on the bank for a while, catching our breath and letting a little reality sink back in. Eventually the sound of the water quieted. I propped myself up on one elbow and looked out at the Canadian. The flash flood appeared to be over, though the water was still extremely high and rushing hard. I looked at the others. Mike was still lying on his back staring up, but it appeared to be shock more than anything. Sam had stopped moaning, though there was a grimace on his face as he probed his ribs with his right hand. I crawled over to him and sat back on my knees, watching him. Eventually he stopped probing and dropped the hand back to his side. I looked a question at him and he shook his head. "I don't think they're broken," he said through gritted teeth. "Bruised 'em up pretty good, though." I nodded. "Yeah, you took a bit of a glancing blow from a steer on the way by," I said. Sam stared at me. "Huh. I don't remember, but that sounds about right." "Do you think you'll be able to ride?" I asked eventually. He shrugged. "Give me a couple hours and I'll give it a try. If I can't, you can rig up a travois for me."

I stood and assessed what was left for us. The herd had bunched on some mountain grass between the river and the tree line, grazing on what they could find there. I walked over and took count. Of the seventy-seven cows we'd left with, only seventeen remained. Even that seemed unimportant now, because I would have to go looking for Fred and I had a very bad feeling about it. I looked for the horses. Both Sam's horses were missing, along with the horse Fred had been riding and Mike's spare horse. We'd packed a few supplies on my spare horse and he had come through, along with Archie. I walked over to the roan I'd borrowed from Jim as a spare and took out the small shovel on his pack. I went over to saddle up Archie and led him past the spot where Sam was lying. Mike looked up and looked away. "I'll be back in an hour or two," I told them.

I led Archie down the bank a short way and mounted up. We followed the bends of the river for a mile or so. There were a few dead cows washed up on the bank here and there, but most seemed to have been carried farther down. If there were any that had survived here and there, we didn't have the resources or supplies to look for them. We'd have to move on. I followed the river another mile or so, noting that the trees were much closer to the river now. I wouldn't be able to ride much farther without going into the river, and both Archie and I had had enough of that to last us for a while. Rounding another bend, there was a huge tree bent low over the water. A large limb extended into the bend of the river, forming a natural barrier. There I saw what I hadn't wanted to see.

Fred lay against the tree limb, his back turned toward me with his head hanging limply over. The red of the shirt he was wearing formed a stark contrast to the brown of the tree limb and the blue-green water rushing by him. I splashed over to him, dismounting and holding the reins in one hand while I checked him over briefly. He was dead. I thought he'd probably been dead for a while before he smashed into the tree limb, but found little consolation in that.

I slipped my rope over his shoulders and pulled him back from the tree. His dead weight was too much for me to lift him onto the horse, given the exertions I'd just been through. I managed to half-drag, half-carry him over and tie his upper body to Archie's saddle. I lifted his legs and guided Archie out of the river. We pulled him back into a small clearing beyond the tree line and I put him down and got the shovel from the saddle.

The shovel wasn't much, but I dug steadily for about forty-five minutes to create a shallow grave where I placed him. I filled the dirt over the grave, carved his name on a thick tree branch I found, and drove that into the ground with the back of the shovel. I said a few words over him and reflected that I would have to find out where he had family when I got back. They would need to be notified. I backed away and looked back at the grave. What I'd done seemed inadequate, but I knew of nothing else to do. Nothing in life had prepared me for something like this. I mounted and rode back to where I'd left Sam and Mike.

I found that Mike had managed to build a small fire to help them dry off and warm up. I walked up, squatted down and held my hands out over the fire. They both looked at me without saying anything. I shook my head. "Fred's gone." We all stared into the fire. Nobody seemed to want to talk about it any further.

Eventually Mike looked and asked if I'd made any plans on what to do from here. I looked at Sam. "Are you able to travel?" He nodded and sat up a little farther, holding his side but not making any noises. "I can," he said. I looked at him skeptically. "We can wait until morning," I told him. "Maybe you'd be better off with a little rest." Sam shook his head emphatically. "No. If we get a decent distance down the trail today, I think we can get home tomorrow, and I'd rather be home." His expression left no room for further discussion. Mike brought Sam's horse over and helped him into the saddle. I kicked dirt over the fire and moved to round up the few cows we had left.

Morning found us at much lower altitudes and working steadily homeward. Having so few cattle made it easier, of course. I couldn't really dwell on the loss right now. It seemed unimportant after burying a man yesterday. I looked around and thought about the difficulties we still faced in getting Sam home. He had hung in the saddle for a few hours yesterday, tying himself into it a one point, and had stayed in it until we made camp. He'd looked a little better this morning, but I didn't think he had a full day in him. We could rig a travois for him, but that would need to be pulled between two horses, with only Mike and me to do that, and we'd need to herd the cattle as well. I looked around at Sam one more time and called a halt.

"I've been thinking," I said conversationally as Mike and Sam rode up to me, "that we've got a small herd that's pretty well trail broken at this point. Horns might just follow along if we're in front. And the rest pretty much follow Horns." Sam could see where I was going and started to shake his head, but Mike restrained him with a hand on the shoulder. "I've got a couple blankets in my bedroll," he said, "and I'll bring a couple long branches. We can be home by tonight." Sam had started to voice his objections, but I could see the idea of getting home had struck a chord with him, and I knew the pain was wearing him down. He allowed me to help him down while Mike set about rigging up the travois. I looked at him sideways. "Still thinking not broken?" I asked finally. Sam shook his head. "Nope. I've had broken ribs before and these ain't broke. Bruised can hurt just about as bad," he admitted finally. I nodded and got up to help Mike set up the travois.

We helped Sam into the travois and set off on the final leg for home. It seemed like we had been gone forever. The trail began to widen and smooth out a little bit, which helped. The cows seemed content to follow. We might need a little luck to make it the rest of the way without the herd being spooked or raided, but maybe we had used up all the bad luck we had for this trip.

Kate rode beside her father as they headed to the north pasture. They had managed to hire a couple hands for a few days, though they could ill afford it, to clean up the aftermath of the slide. They'd hauled some big rocks off to the side, and had dragged the dead cows to the far western edge of the pasture. The scavengers were doing their job. That was about all she and Jim could do about the carcasses. The mud would settle into the ground and the pasture would recover. They pulled up and sat their horses at the edge of the slide area, watching as the last few rocks were hauled. Jim paid the hands and asked them to stick around long enough to help him drive the herd back up to the north pasture. Kate followed them back down, unsaddled her horse and went back into the house.

She sat at the kitchen table, watching through the window as the herd was pushed toward the upper pasture. It had been several days now since she'd hoped Chance would return with others and with the herd. There was no way to send or receive any news and she couldn't make the time go any faster. Her mind returned again to the strange story of how her mother had disappeared and how the soldier named Gibson had buried a large shipment of gold coins. She had a feeling her mother had told her father a little more about that before she left, but Kate knew that Jim wouldn't discuss it any further. No matter, she thought, we have what we need here without it.

Kate got up and walked out to sweep off the front porch. Activity of any kind was better than sitting around, wondering where Chance was. She righted a flower pot that had tipped over and picked up the broom from the corner. As had become her habit, she looked up to check the trail to Cimarron. They could look down that trail for a short distance from the porch. She froze and shielded her eyes from the setting sun with her hand. She wasn't imagining. There was a very small herd coming down the trail. She looked for the riders and saw only two. There should have been four. Her eyes dropped and she saw a third being pulled on a travois. Kate dropped the broom and left the porch at a dead run.

Chapter Six

Home at Last

I knew we were a little rag-tag group coming down the trail towards home. We'd had to drive the herd through town in Cimarron to get to this trail leading us down the final stretch. I hadn't wanted to stop and discuss things with anybody. The mayor and a couple others had come out and I'd summarized briefly for them. Mayor Purvis had volunteered to find out what he could about Fred's family and get in touch with them. I gratefully accepted. It was one thing lifted from my plate. I'd told him as best I could where I had buried Fred.

Sam had climbed up onto the saddle to ride through Cimarron, but he was back in the travois now. The doctor hadn't been in his office, but we'd managed to leave word, asking him to come out and tend to Sam at the Randolph house first chance he had. We rode on past my ranch. I didn't have enough cows now to maintain a separate herd, and I felt sure Jim would be agreeable to me joining mine up with his. I turned my head to the right as we rode past the edge of my property line. There seemed to be a number of trees down and many pools of standing water. There must have been a lot of rain since we'd left, I reflected.

I heard my name being called. I swung back around and saw Kate coming down the trail at full speed. I managed to dismount before she launched herself into my arms. I staggered back against my horse, got my balance and returned the embrace. A couple "I love you" declarations were whispered back and forth. I was home and the sunshine had broken through the clouds for the first time in many days. For the first time since the disaster at the Canadian river, my spirits lifted and I felt confident that good things were still ahead.

We stayed that way for some time, until finally I realized I was hearing rasping noises to my left. Sam was harrumphing. "When you two are finished, any chance you could get this sick man inside and make him a little more comfortable?" Kate disengaged herself and ran around to kneel beside Sam, offering encouragement and promising to take care of him. I shook my head and grinned. That's what the old codger had been after the whole time. Well, he'd earned some rest time. Kate came around and swung up behind me on Archie. We proceeded on to the Randolph place. I could see Jim riding in from the south pasture. He took in my explanation in a moment and recruited Mike to help him drive my cows up to join his in the north pasture. I turned back and helped Sam to the sofa in the house. Kate brought him some brandy and he seemed to fall asleep instantly.

Kate took me by the hand and led me out to the kitchen. We held hands across the table and she asked me what had happened. I told her in only a few sentences about the trip out and the purchase of the cows. Dodge City stories could wait for another day. I relived for a moment the scene at the river crossing and Fred's death. When I'd finished, she came around and wrapped her arms around me, her head resting on my shoulder. "I pretty much spent everything I had left," I said. "I don't know how long it will take to get a herd going now." I felt her nodding her head. "It's OK," she said. "You're home and safe. We'll figure out the rest of it."

Kate sat on the back porch and watched her father as he worked on saddle breaking a new horse in the corral. Chance had gone into town in Cimarron to get some building supplies and food after spending the night in his sleeping bag on the floor in their living room. Sam remained on the sofa, sleeping intermittently. Doc Charles had come that morning to examine him, and as Sam had suspected, he miraculously had only some bruised ribs. Recovery should come quickly. Considering all they'd been through with the flood waters, they really had a lot to be thankful for, even though she knew how deep Chance's feelings ran—both hurt at Fred's death and the blow to his hopes for establishing a working ranch.

A door she'd closed in her mind just a few days ago had been opened again. She'd seen Chance's disappointment at losing the seed money for their ranch. She knew it was hard just to make enough for the established, working ranch she had with her father. She suspected that Chance may have already entertained in his mind the idea of mining in the Sangre de Cristo Mountains again, as he had done before. The gold he'd found and mined then had given him the money for the ranch property and the herd he'd just lost. She didn't want him to go. It was dangerous and he'd been lucky the first time. It might not turn out nearly so well if he went the second time. She suspected he was a little reluctant to go, anyway. He had more to lose this time.

She watched as her father began unsaddling the mare he'd been breaking. She felt certain he knew more about the money buried by the soldier, Gibson. She'd known him all her life and felt certain he'd avoided talking more on purpose. She'd been reluctant to push the subject any further, knowing there was probably still some pain surrounding her mother's disappearance, and the money hadn't seemed that important. But now it could save Chance from making a more dangerous trip into the mountains for gold mining. Besides that, she needed a certain amount of closure about what had happened to her mother.

Jim came up the path toward the house. He'd been up and working for six or seven hours already and she knew he'd be coming in for lunch. As he climbed the stairs, Kate remained where she was instead of getting up to join him in the kitchen. The break in routine gave him pause, and he stopped to give her a questioning look. "Dad," she said, "I need to talk a little more about the time when mom disappeared and about the coins buried by the soldier, Gibson." Jim stared at her heavily for a moment, then nodded in resignation and sat down next to her on the porch.

I pushed through the doors at Purvis' General Store, carrying the first of two loads of supplies I'd bought. This load was the building materials. I dropped some boards, a basket of nails and a few other items on a small wagon I'd borrowed from Jim to rig up behind Archie. The second load was food, so I went back into the store, brushing past a guy I'd never seen before, which was a little unusual for me in Cimarron, though there were a fair number of people passing through the town from time to time. This one wore a battered old felt hat and had a pair of boots that had seen better days, heavily scuffed and run down at the heels. He wore two guns tied down, which we didn't see that much around here.

I was headed for the counter to pick up my bags of flour and salt when I noticed a small section of the store that looked new to me. It held some mining supplies. Tim's Mining Supply store had long since moved to Denver. A few folks passed through on their way to the Sangre de Cristo Mountains so it made some sense to carry a few mining materials in the general store. I'd been thinking about mining gold very lately myself, though I was very reluctant to discuss it with Kate. I stopped and looked at what he'd stocked. I still had a pick, a mesh box for sifting the ore and a couple other things I'd used the summer before. The one thing I knew I was out of—mercury. I saw a bottle of it on the shelf and paused. On impulse I picked it up and took it back to the counter. "Let's add this, Dave," I said, placing it on the counter. Purvis' eyebrows raised in a question mark but he said nothing as I reached into my pocket for a couple more coins. I placed the bottle on top of the food sacks, feeling the stranger's eye on me as I walked back through the store, loaded the wagon and pointed Archie toward the ranch.

Kyle Moore drifted out of the store, pausing at the railing outside to shield his eyes against the sun as he watched the buggy wheeling out of town. He'd been in Cimarron only two days and had begun to lose interest in the town. He'd been drifting west for a couple months now, leaving Texas after the law began to show too much interest in a couple of shootings he'd been involved with. There had been a stagecoach robbery a few weeks back, teaming up with a couple drifters who were now at the saloon down the street. He knew their names only as Murchison and Duke. He was pretty sure the names weren't real, but then, neither was his. The buggy disappeared down the road and he moved back toward the saloon, not wanting to be too noticeable around town. He'd cased it for a couple days now. There didn't appear to be a sheriff, though there was a town jail. The jail didn't appear to be currently in use. He had sized up the bank in town and thought it would be pretty easy to rob. From the activity he'd seen coming and going, though, he thought it probably wasn't worth it.

He paused outside the saloon for a moment before going back in to rejoin the other two. The only use he knew of for mercury was in processing gold, and the stranger in the buggy had bought some before leaving. None of the other supplies suggested gold mining, but robbing one man of his gold would be easy and maybe worth the while. He thought about the two inside who had helped him on the stage robbery. They were expendable and he wouldn't hesitate to leave them behind or get rid of them if needed, but maybe they could serve some purpose for a while. He didn't want to draw any attention to himself, but they could keep an eye on the dark-haired man with the wagon, who looked like a rancher but bought mining supplies. It was worth another day or two around this town.

I stared at the newspaper clipping in front of me, then across the table at Jim and Kate. The date on the article was from the time when I'd lived here in Cimarron with my father. The clipping told the story of a shipment of money lost to an Apache raid a little north of here. Two soldiers had buried the gold and escaped the raid. One had died before reaching Fort Stanton, but the other had successfully reached the fort. I looked first at Kate, then at Jim, uncomprehending. Kate reached across the table and took my hand. "The soldier who made it to the fort was named George Gibson. We know this because he left the fort and showed up at our doorstep several weeks later. He stayed with us a short while.

Mother left here about ten days after he left." I switched my stare over to Jim who only nodded quietly.

Kate continued the story. "George Gibson was killed shortly after he left here. There was a subsequent news article, and Dad knew someone at Fort Stanton who confirmed that they found Gibson's body. There was no sign of a woman with him, and no sign of the buried treasure." I processed that one for a moment. "So," I said eventually, "you don't really know what became of your mother, or for that matter, what became of the gold coins." Kate studied her hands on the table for a short while. "You're mostly right," she said eventually. "Dad, tell Chance the rest of it. What you told me earlier today."

Jim was clearly reluctant to talk. He took a couple sips of the water in front of him. "Anne—Kate's mother—," he explained, "at first found his to be an interesting story, and she repeated to me the things he was saying to her, though I don't think she believed them at first. He seemed down on his luck and pretty beat up from his experiences, so we planned at first to let him stay a short while for some work on the ranch. Then we'd tell him to be on his way." His voice gained a little strength as he talked. "As time went by, Anne seemed more and more taken by this Gibson fellow and his story of gold and good times in San Francisco. At first Anne would confide in me the things he was telling her. But eventually, she became quiet about him. When he left, she barely talked to me until the day she left. I'm not sure if she went to meet up with him, but I'm afraid she might have."

Jim left off talking and I cleared my throat to speak, but Kate stopped me by placing her hand on top of mine. "There's a little more," she told me. I sat back and looked at Jim one more time. "Before she ran away from here," Jim said, "and before she stopped talking about Gibson to me, she told me he had told her where the gold is buried." I sat in stunned silence and waited. "According to

Anne, Gibson said the money is a few miles off the trail between here and the Raton Pass. He claimed that if you follow that trail across the Canadian River, probably not far from where you forded, and continue toward Raton, there is a huge pine tree split by lightning at the mouth of a small trail leading off to the west northwest. A couple miles up that trail, it ends abruptly at a cliff face. There is a small cave in the cliff face near the end of the trail Gibson told Anne they buried the gold in a pile of rocks toward the back the that cave. He says he carved a crescent moon symbol into the rock near the entrance to the cave."

I sat back and tried to choose which question I wanted to ask first. Finally, one formed in my mind. I looked at Kate. "Why are you telling me this story? Are you expecting me to go after the treasure?" I looked at Jim. "Have you looked for it?" Jim shook his head. "I haven't" he said. I switched my gaze back to Kate and waited. She leaned forward and took my face between her hands. "I'm worried you're thinking about going back to mine in the Sangre de Cristo Mountains because you've lost the herd." One look at my face probably told her she was right. "It's too dangerous," she said. "It isn't worth it. I can't lose you." I considered that one and thought about the mercury bottle I had over at my house. "OK," I said after a while. "I promise I won't go back to the Sangre de Cristos. What about this buried money?" I lapsed into thought for a moment. "Gibson's gold. What about that?"

Kate sat back and looked at me. She teared up a little. "I want you to be safe, but I want you to be happy too. If you just have to do something to recover the herd, I'd rather you stay closer to home and look for the buried money. I'm still scared for what might happen, but at least it's something other than mining again." My mind began to churn with the possibilities. Compared to what we'd just done trying to buy the herd and drive it home through a flash flood, this didn't seem too bad. And the potential reward was great. I looked at Jim. "You told me you've never looked for it, but you didn't say why. I don't want to stir up painful memories. Did you not want to look because of how Anne might fit in to the story?" Jim looked away. "That's part of it," he said. "There's another reason." He stopped and told another sip of the water. "I haven't told you this either, Kate," he said in a small voice. "There was a story that made the rounds that said the trail to the gold leads through a Jicarilla sacred burial ground."

As Jim's words hung in the air and I struggled to absorb them, Kate turned to me and said, "Chance, if you go, I'm going with you."

Chapter Seven

On Gibson's Trail

The discussions and back and forth talks about the buried gold coins went on for pretty much a week. It began with a question of whether or not the gold, if it was still there, could be found with only a description of twenty-year-old landmarks. Would the pine tree still be there, or would the lightning strike have so weakened it that it would be dead and long gone? Would the trail leading to the cave still be there, or would it be grown over from lack of use? The easiest question was about the half moon etched on the cliff wall by Gibson before leaving. That, we decided, would likely still be there because no one would have a reason to remove it, and rain running over it wouldn't be likely to erode it. As to the first two questions about landmarks and the trail, the only way to know for sure would be to look for it.

The sacred burial ground, if Jim was right about that, would be a much bigger concern. I needed to check with Sam about that, but I wanted to give him a chance for some rest. I had asked around town quite a bit for the last week, and I knew that with regards to the native Jicarilla Apache tribe, things were not as scary for the settlers around here as they had been back when the gold was lost in 1859. When Gibson and his squad were attacked, there had been a large battle with U.S troops just five years before. Two battles in fact, with the Apaches and some Ute warriors defeating a force of about sixty soldiers in the first battle. A second detachment was sent, with Kit Carson as a guide, to pursue the Jicarilla warriors. After a winter of pursuit, a peace agreement was made with the Apache chiefs, but not all the warriors had agreed to it. Many small bands had dispersed. No doubt Gibson's squad had run into one of them. Talks had been under way for a few years now about establishing a reservation for them, but again, not all were agreed. So, while it didn't seem as big a concern as it had been back then, it was definitely not something to take lightly.

I sat on my porch, taking a break from the ongoing work I was doing to replace the broken boards on the northern side, where the house had taken the hardest blows from the winter storms of the past twenty years. I thought about what I knew about the buried money and the dangers I was aware of in trying to retrieve it. Kate was agreeable to my going, but only on the condition she could come with me. That was the one we hadn't worked out. I thought it was much too dangerous to take her with me, and she insisted she would be with me if I went. I sighed, went out to saddle Archie, and headed over to the Randolph house. Maybe we could talk this one out yet.

We sat around the dinner table in the Randolph kitchen, and it was probably the most quiet and uncomfortable session we'd had around that table. I had repeated what I'd learned about the situation with the Apaches in that area—that it wasn't as dangerous as it had been twenty years before. That didn't seem to be helping. Finally, in the developing silence, I asked Kate why she insisted on coming with me. "Is there anything besides you worrying about my safety?" I asked. "I can find someone to come with me and watch my back. I don't understand why it has to be you."

"I think it has something to do with my mother," she said finally. Jim and I both looked turned to look at her. This was something we hadn't covered in all the prior discussions. I sat quietly and waited. "I can't shake the feeling that she was up there the last that anybody knew. If you are going to that cave, I need to see for myself. I need to put this to rest in my mind. I know there's probably nothing to find, other than the gold coins, if that's really there. I know they didn't find any trace of her. I just need to put this to rest in my mind." She turned to Jim. "Dad, I know you must have thought about this. I know you had me to take care of and couldn't do anything else all those years ago. But don't you wonder sometimes? Isn't there some part of you that wants to take a look?"

Jim's eyes dropped to the table. There was another long and uncomfortable silence. "Yes," he finally said simply. "I wondered a thousand times about her. Did she survive? If so, did she ever want to come back? Did she never meet with Gibson and simply ride west? If that happened, would we really have never heard from her again?" He rubbed the back of his neck absent-mindedly. "You're right, Kate, you were only four years old and I had to be there for you. I couldn't leave you with anyone here and I couldn't put myself in that much danger." He left off in mid-thought, stood, turned and looked out the window. "For what it's worth, my friend at the fort confirmed there's no owner of that shipment still alive," he said absent-mindedly. "He wouldn't explain that to me." Kate's eyes were directed at her father's back as he stood at the window.

"Would you come too, then?" she asked. Without turning, Jim simply said "Yes."

Well, that put the whole thing back in my lap. I wasn't feeling any better about it than before, and began to say so. Jim turned back from the window and sat down again, putting his hand on my arm. "Chance, let me say something now. I know you love my daughter and I can't tell you how happy that makes me. As far as I'm concerned, you're already the son I never had and nothing would make me happier than for you to be with Kate. I can't tell you how much I appreciate your concern for her safety." He paused to let the words sink in. I glanced up at Kate and saw the tears in her eyes. Jim continued. "I've lived a little longer than either of you, and here's something I've learned: sometimes you have to compromise a little. Kate needs to put this to rest. You lost your mother too, but you buried her years ago. Kate didn't have that kind of finality. Her mother just rode away. She badly needs to put this to rest if she can. I'm not happy about the danger either, but Kate needs this. I'll come and watch out for the both of you, and you can watch out for me. We'll do it together. What do you say?"

There was a lump in my throat too big for me to swallow, it seemed. I tried to answer a couple times, but the words didn't want to come. Finally, I nodded. "OK," I said. "We'll do it together."

Kate rose from the table, leaned over and wrapped her arms around me, head buried on my shoulder. I could feel her tears on my neck. "Thank you," she whispered. I could only nod. Jim cleared his throat, hesitated, then left the room quietly.

Kyle Moore sat in the saloon, staring expectantly across the table. "Well?" He had trouble remembering which one was Murchison and which one was Duke. He thought this one was Murchison. It didn't really matter to him. "Where's your friend?" he asked. Murchison shrugged. "Reilly stopped at the general store. Duke hung around to see what he's getting. We trailed him to a ranch north of town. Nice spread, but not many cows. We watched him for a day. Nothing special. Works on the house. Seems to share a spread with a neighbor. Watches the herd over there on the other ranch. Goes over there for meals. Looks like he's sweet on the neighbor lady. I think it's a waste of time to stay here."

Moore glared at him. "I'll take care of any thinking we need." He drained the last of his beer and motioned for another. "Let's see what he bought at the general store. Any sign he might be going on a trip?" Murchison furrowed his brow for a moment. "Maybe. He got a wagon from the neighbor and started throwing a few things in there this morning." He looked around and waved for a beer. Moore sat back and thought this over. "Anything that looked like mining equipment?" Murchison chugged his beer and shook his head. "Nope. Maybe a pick, but nothing else. Mostly looked like food." He wiped his mouth with the back of his sleeve and looked around for his next beer.

The batwing doors opened and Duke came in, pulling back a chair and sitting down heavily. Moore looked at him expectantly. "Well?" "He's on his way over here, I think" Duke answered. "He bought some supplies like he's maybe going on a trip. Food you can pack, stuff like that. Nothing you'd use for mining, though." Moore had already made up his mind in spite of this new report. "We'll stick around for a couple days. We've got nothing else going on. If he leaves town, follow him for a while, then one of you can come back and tell me what's going on. I've got a feeling about this one." Murchison and Duke both shrugged. The doors opened again and

Chance Reilly came in. They all fell silent and looked at the table as he passed by.

I completed my purchases and threw the things I'd bought, mostly food for the trail, into the back of Jim's wagon. I watched idly as another stranger I'd never seen came out of the store and headed for the saloon. I climbed on the wagon and drove a couple blocks down to Sam's place, tied it up, and went inside. Sam waved me to a table as I came in. "He shoved a beer at me and grimaced slightly, taking a seat across the table from me. "How's the ribs?" I asked. I knew he'd spent several days off his feet, which was unheard of from Sam. He only nodded and said, "Coming along." I knew that was all I would get out of him on the subject.

I changed direction and asked him about what I had planned on asking him about. "Have you ever heard a story about a soldier named George Gibson and a lost shipment of gold coins?" I asked him abruptly. Sam had been staring at three guys at a table across the room, and I guess I caught him off guard. He looked at me vacantly for a second, refocusing on me and turning the question over in his mind. "Yeah, sure," he said. "There've been at least a dozen fools out there digging around in the mountains, looking for that gold. Haven't seen any in the last ten years or so, though. Nobody has any idea where it is, and everybody concerned has been dead for twenty years." He looked at me with a growing comprehension in his eyes. "Don't tell me…"

I hunched over and nodded slightly. "Here's what…" Sam stopped me with a hand over my arm. "Not just yet," he said, looking back at the table across the room. "Something's not right about those three. They've been hanging around here and hanging around town for a few days now, and I don't know what they're here for. They took a little too much interest when you came in. My nose tells me they are trouble. Wait till they're gone before we talk." With that he got up and went back behind the bar. I nursed my beer for a half hour until the three of them got up and left.

I waited another five minutes for Sam to get freed up at the bar, then he came over to rejoin me. I glanced over at the table where the three men had been. "Who are they?" I asked. Sam shook his head. "Nobody seems to know and that's part of the problem. They're pretty secretive. They also seem a little too interested in watching you." That one only surprised me a little. It did seem that one of them was always in the general store when I bought anything. For the life of me, though, I didn't know what they would be interested in. They couldn't possibly know about the money. I shrugged it off and changed the subject back to what I'd come in to talk about. "About that gold shipment," I began. I glanced up for his reaction. Sam simply sat back, expressionless. "I may have a pretty good idea where it is." Now he registered surprise.

I told him the entire story, starting with the part he already knew about the loss of the coins and the two survivors. It turned out Sam hadn't heard of the death of Campbell on the way back to Ft. Stanton, but he knew there hadn't been any survivors in the long run to tell where the gold might be. The part about the disappearance of Anne Randolph and what she'd told Jim before leaving, was, of course, news to Sam. As I recounted the story, Sam mostly looked at the wall behind me, occasionally switching his gaze back to me and nodding, letting me know he was still listening. Finally, I finished the story and sat back, waiting for his reaction.

He absently traced a crack in the table with his forefinger, and seemed to be considering a few things to say before changing his mind and lapsing back into silence. Finally, he simply looked up and said "So, you're going after the gold?" "I think so," I told him. I explained the compromise I'd reached with Kate and Jim. Sam winced when I said that Kate was planning to go, but eventually nodded when I explained the reasons. "There's only one thing that could still stop me," I said. "What do you know about the story that there's a Jicarilla Apache burial ground up there? That might make the difference between risky and downright foolish. I don't think I would mess with that."

Sam considered his answer, then shook his head no. "I don't think that one's true. You know how stories kind of grow with time and get all kinds of things added in. I didn't hear anything about a sacred burial ground until a couple or three years after Gibson was found dead. I don't put much stock in it." I felt a little relief flow through me. "In that case, I think it's on." I rose to go, but Sam stopped me with a final question. "What about the mother. What about Anne Randolph? Are you looking for her too?" I shook my head. "If we run across any clues, we'll do what we can. Nobody's expecting to find any, not even Kate." Sam rose, shook my hand, and told me to stop in on my way out of town. I went outside and mounted up.

Sam walked across the saloon and watched through the window as Chance rode away. All three of the men who'd been hanging out in his saloon were lounging against the hitching rail across the street. Their eyes followed Chance as he rode out of town.

We gathered in the yard at Kate and Jim's house. Mike was there, getting a few last-minute instructions about taking care of the place while we were gone. Neither Jim nor I was really concerned. Mike seemed very capable of taking care of things for a few days. Jim and I both had a pack horse besides the ones we were riding. We had supplies to last us for a week, maybe longer if we went easy on the food or killed a deer. None of us wanted this to turn into an extended trip. We went out through the gate and stayed together for a short way down the trail to town, then we split up as planned. Natural caution told me not to ride through town all together, advertising we were on some kind of trip which would leave the ranches empty. Jim and Kate would take the longer way around Cimarron and we'd meet up on the other side after I had a few last words with Sam on the way out.

Upon reaching town, I rode up and dismounted in front of the saloon. We'd gotten away a little later than planned, but it was still only about ten o'clock and I knew the bar wouldn't be open for business. Sam came out to meet me on the porch and asked if Mike was squared away at the ranch. I told him everything was taken care of, but it might not hurt if Sam checked in after a couple days. Sam nodded absently, his eyes sweeping up and down the street. After a few glances up and down, he asked if I could let him know the general route we'd be taking. That surprised me a little, but I told him we would follow the general path we'd taken with the cattle, crossing the Canadian River pretty much where we'd crossed a few weeks before. After that, we would be searching for a small trail back toward the cliffs. Sam shook my hand, wished me luck and watched as I rode off. That had seemed a little strange, but Sam did have his unique ways sometimes. I kicked Archie into a trot as I left town.

Sam stayed on the porch for a few minutes, then went inside for a broom, came back out and pretended to sweep the porch for a while. He didn't have to wait long. In a short while, two of the three strangers who had been hanging around town drifted down the street, picking up the pace a little as they followed Chance from a distance. Sam put the broom down against the wall of the saloon, lost in thought. He pondered his possible courses of action as he went back inside.

Chapter Eight

Hunters and the Hunted

I trotted Archie out of town, both relieved by Sam's take on the burial ground question and puzzled by all his questions on where we were going and how we would get there. He wasn't in shape yet to join us, in my opinion, and he didn't seem to want to do that anyway. I puzzled over his motives for asking. Maybe I should have just asked him outright, but he was far too cagey to tell anything he didn't want to talk about.

I reached the meeting point where this road merged with the trail taken around town by Jim and Kate, pulled off the road and let Archie graze while I rested under a tree. The other thing I'd never really gotten comfortable with was having Kate along on the trip. What if she were to be captured by someone? Most men in the West were respectful of women, but it was still a pretty wild place in many areas, and there was no predicting the Apaches. I brooded over that one for a few minutes, then glanced up to see two men on horseback coming around a turn in the road. They seemed to hesitate when they saw me, then continued to ride forward. As they drew closer, I could see they were two of the men Sam had been so suspicious of in the saloon. I watched and stood up as they approached my position. I rested one hand near my gun, cautious but not threatening. They seemed to avoid eye contact until they came alongside, then nodded briefly and rode on without saying anything. I continued to watch until they disappeared around a bend in the road, then sat back down. That seemed a little strange on the whole, but at least they were leaving town, or so it seemed.

Relaxing in the shade of the tree, I guess I must have dozed off. The next thing I knew, I was sleepily scratching a persistent itch on my left ear. After brushing at it a few times, my eyes came open to see Kate kneeling beside me, tickling my ear with a leaf. She grinned. "Fine watchman you are," she teased. "General Grant and half the Union army could have come through here and you wouldn't know it." "Nah, not half the army. Quarter, maybe." I stood and pulled her up beside me. Funny how my pulse rate seemed to go up when she was that close. Jim just chuckled and tightened his saddle, which probably didn't need it.

I recounted my conversation with Sam, emphasizing his questions about our route and Jim only nodded appreciatively. "What am I missing?" I finally asked. "You told him how long we expected this to take, right?" I nodded. "Well," said Jim, "if we aren't back after about eight or nine days, I'll bet this new pair of boots I'm wearing that Sam will come looking for us. I'm pretty glad he's backing us up." Realization dawned on me. I actually felt a little foolish for not thinking of it myself. "His ribs, though...". I stopped before finishing the thought. If Sam decided to come after us, you'd have to tie him down to keep him at home. "Sam is as tough as old boot leather," Kate reminded me. She patted my arm. "Besides, after another week he'll be in much better shape."

Well, both those statements were true. I even grinned a little when I thought about Sam coming to get us. You could bet he'd be packing that old double-barreled shotgun. I chuckled a little as I swung up into the saddle. Jim and Kate laughed a little too, maybe seeing the same mental image as me. Then we headed up the trail in search of Gibson's gold.

Murchison and Duke were dismounted and standing in a thick cover of trees, just up the way from a bend in the trail that had obscured them from Reilly's view after they had passed by. They hadn't expected him to be stopped and dismounted, so they were startled after coming around a curve and seeing him sitting, leaning against a tree and watching them. Instinctively realizing how suspicious it would look to turn back, they had continued past him, then had taken cover off the trail as soon as they could. When they heard hoofbeats coming up the road toward them, they each soothed and quieted their horses, trying to prevent any possible noise.

The party came around the bend, and Murchison and Duke stared in surprise to see not just Chance Reilly, but three riders, talking as they passed by. They were too far away to pick up any of the conversation. They both remained motionless, far back in the trees. Finally, the riders moved out of sight. There had been two pack horses as well as the three riders and their horses. Each stood in silence for a moment before beginning to lead their horses out of the trees and back to the trail.

Duke finally broke the silence. "That was the neighbor, Randolph, and his daughter, right?" "Yup." Murchison continued to stare up the road before turning and mounting. "Well," persisted Duke, "whaddya think of that?" Murchison chewed on the wad of tobacco in his mouth for a moment before spitting onto the road. "Don't know," he finally admitted. "This just got more interesting, though. Maybe Moore was onto something after all. You noticed they had pack horses, right?" Duke nodded in agreement as he mounted his horse. "Do you think I need to go back to Moore and report this?" Murchison turned that one over in his mind a few times. "No. I don't think so. We don't know that much just yet. Let's follow a while longer and see if we can figure out what they're doing." He nudged his horse forward and Duke followed suit. They would be a little more careful when coming around the turns in the trail from now on.

Sam waited and watched for the third man, who hadn't been with the other two when they rode out of town this morning. The third one must fancy himself a gunfighter, Sam reflected, because he wore two tied down guns. Most times that was just for show, he knew. Most couldn't shoot straight with the opposite hand if their life depended on it. Then again, Sam thought grimly, sometimes their lives had depended on it and it hadn't turned out too well. Maybe this guy was an exception and maybe he wasn't. The smart ones didn't advertise their expertise with guns.

About 12:30 in the afternoon Sam carried a pan of dishwater outside and tossed the water onto the dusty main street. As he turned to go back inside, he saw the third man lounging on a bench outside the hotel down the street. He was leaning back, hat tipped down, feigning sleep. About an hour later, he showed up in the saloon, nursed two beers for about two hours, then left. A check down the street told Sam he was back on the bench, simply watching the horses and wagons going by in the street. He was waiting for one or both of his saddle buddies to come back, Sam thought. As long as that was the case, Sam decided he would wait here too. He checked the street frequently. If the man left, or certainly if the other two came back and they all left, Sam would be following.

With that thought in mind, he stepped into the back room of the saloon and began pulling together a few items, starting with his old double-barreled shotgun and several boxes of shells. He pulled out a rifle along with ammunition for it and put that in the pile also. Just then the door opened and his nephew Lenny came in, carrying a couple boxes full of whiskey they'd had delivered that morning. Lenny set the box down, eyed the pile of weaponry on the floor and looked up at his uncle. "Going hunting?" he asked finally. "You might say that," Sam answered evasively. "Or I might not go at all. I'll let you know if I do." Lenny shrugged and pulled the door open. He glanced back and left without any further questions. He pretty much knew he'd gotten all the answers he would get. Sam smiled to himself and stepped over the pile of guns and ammo. Maybe he would pick up a little trail food at the store as well.

A hard day's ride would get us close to the Canadian River crossing. We weren't going to cross in anything other than full daylight after my earlier experience, so we planned to make camp two hours or so this side of the river.

Kate fell in beside me as Jim rode point for most of the trip. She had seemed a little subdued since we'd met up. After a little small talk about the trip, she asked "What do you think Sam was worried about?" I told her about the men hanging out in the saloon. "Sam felt the three of them were up to no good, and seemed to show a little too much interest in what I was doing. The thing is, I don't see how they could possibly know about this trip or what we're doing. If they are still in town when we get back, which I doubt, I'll see what else I can find out about them." She seemed happy with that plan of action, and we rode in companionable silence for a while. She showed me once again how uncomfortably good she was at reading my mind when she asked, "You're worried for me, aren't you—about my safety on this trip?" "I am," I admitted. She nodded and we rode along a little farther. "What worries you the most?" she asked. I thought about that one. "I think," I said eventually, "it has been the talk about your mother and all of us wondering if the Apaches could have taken her. I don't know how I could live with myself if that happened to you. I don't know if I could track you and find you. I can't imagine how helpless that would feel." "How can I make that better?" she asked. "If you thought you could follow and find me, would that help? Would you worry less?"

It was hard to imagine feeling better about the scenario we were talking about, but I supposed something was better than nothing. If I could follow and find her, I would have a chance to do something about it. "Yes," I said eventually, "I hate the thought of what we're talking about, but I suppose that would help." Kate reached over and patted my hand. "I'll think about that one," she told me, "now let's talk about something happier." That suited me just fine. We began talking about our plans for the ranch and what we would do with the money if we found it. My spirits rose again as we talked about it, and I thought now, for the hundredth time, how lucky I was to have found this new family.

As the sun began to drop and afternoon faded into evening, we decided to make camp. I estimated we were a couple hours from the Canadian River crossing, which was our goal for the day. We judged that we were far enough from any hostile territory to have a small campfire for the evening, but it would be a luxury we wouldn't have again until we returned this way at the end of the trip. We pulled off the trail into a small clearing, arranged a circle of stones around the campfire and pulled a log a comfortable distance away from the fire. After dinner, I gathered up our food and hung it over a tree limb a short distance from the camp. Jim spread out his blankets a few yards away from the fire and turned in early. Kate sat on the log, and seemed to be whittling, of all things.

I sat near her with my back propped up against the log and watched what she was doing. She had gathered maybe a dozen small sticks and was removing a small band of bark near the middle of each stick. When she had done so for all the sticks, she gathered them up and sat down next to me. "It's a little colder than I thought," she said, gathering up both our blankets and wrapping them around us. She snuggled up next to me. My pulse rate was doing what it usually did in these situations. "I guess you're wondering about these sticks," she began. Right, the sticks. Actually, I had forgotten all about them, but this brought me back to the present.

"Sure," I said, "tell me about the sticks." She chuckled softly. There was that mind reading thing again. "OK, you said you would feel better if you thought you could find me if I was taken, right?" "Right." "Well," she resumed, "that's what these are for. I have about eight or ten of these, with the bark cut off on a section of each of them. I've put them in a small pocket I have on the inside of this coat. If I were taken and my hands were free, or maybe even if they were tied in front of me, I think I could reach the pocket and drop one of these sticks to mark a fork in the trail or a change of direction. I don't think they would raise any suspicion."

I took one of the sticks and looked at it more closely, then at the pocket in her jacket. It did seem like a possible help if the worst occurred. Two thoughts struck me at once: that it was very smart thinking, number one, and that she had done it for me, not for her. She wasn't motivated by worry about herself, but by concern for me and the fact that I worried for her. It was a downright humbling thought that a woman this wonderful cared so much for me. She reached over, took the stick and put it back in her pocket. I leaned forward and threw some dirt over the fire, then leaned back with my head propped up against the log. Kate laid her head on my shoulder, and we drifted off to sleep.

Murchison and Duke trailed slowly, relying more on tracks now, instead of sound. Keeping them in sight wouldn't be possible if they were to escape detection. If they were seen again, Reilly would certainly realize they had circled back around to follow him. The trail seemed to be heading toward the Canadian River, but they felt pretty sure there wouldn't be a crossing tonight. That gave them the luxury of following slowly without worrying that their quarry would get away. The farther they went, the more difficult it was going to be to report back to Moore. Each had a certain fear of Kyle Moore that they didn't want to admit. There was a coldness about him, to begin with. There was also his bragging about the men he'd killed in gunfights. They didn't know how much to believe, but neither wanted to put him to the test.

As the afternoon wore on and dusk approached, the danger of overtaking Reilly and the others became too great. They had no idea of the destination, so they couldn't afford to be seen yet. After a little discussion, they dismounted and led the horses forward on foot. They could take as long as they needed to find the campsite unobserved. Though they knew they were losing ground as long as the others rode, this, they decided, was the safest way. In the end, their noses told them when to stop. The smell of the campfire reached them. They led the horses off the trail and proceeded carefully through the underbrush. Luckily recent rains had kept the brush and sticks moist, lessening the noise that came with walking over dry leaves and sticks. When they could see the campfire through the trees, they retreated about fifty yards and quietly set up their own camp. They could smell the meat roasting at the other camp, but they couldn't afford to have a fire. Dinner consisted of beans out of a can.

Moore would be getting antsy, they knew, about not hearing from them, but there was nothing to report yet. They agreed that Duke would leave for Cimarron by noon tomorrow with whatever news they had to report. They then conversed in low tones about how to resume following the trail tomorrow. They couldn't afford to let Reilly slip away in the morning undetected. It was agreed that they would each take a watch during the night. Duke would stay up until midnight, at which time Murchison would relieve him by taking the watch until six. By six, if not sooner, they would both be up and ready to follow. They would have to play it by ear as far as how they could meet up again after Duke went back to report to Moore. Hopefully there would be a landmark for a rendezvous, and they would have to agree on a time to meet there. They really needed to know where Reilly was going. The sooner the better.

As Murchison turned in, he idly considered the packhorses, the secrecy of the trip, and whether or not he might try to double-cross the other two if Reilly and his friends came back with something valuable. He was inclined not to, but he would keep his eyes open. Duke he could handle, but he didn't want Kyle Moore following him for the rest of his life. Another thought struck him, causing his eyes to pop wide open. What did Moore know that he hadn't told them, and was Moore setting them up for a double-cross of his own? He closed his eyes but tossed for a long time before drifting off to sleep.

Chapter Nine

Landmarks and Decisions

We'd reached the Canadian a little later than I'd expected. We'd had a good early start at sunrise, but it was close to midday by the time we reached the river. We were dismounted and standing on the bank now. I was watching the water rush by and remembering our fateful crossing with the cattle just a few weeks ago. Jim and Kate watched me from the corner of their eyes. I glanced downstream a bit, knowing I had recently buried Fred just a mile or two down this same river bank. I became aware of the two of them watching me, saying nothing, and resolved to pull myself together. The river was still high and running pretty hard, but it was nothing like it had been, and we weren't trying to drive a herd of cattle across with a wagon following.

I walked around to my packhorse and took down a long, stout rope. "One request," I said. We all hang on to this rope as we cross. Take a good turn or two around your hand with it. You can let go if you're getting dragged downstream by it, but you have something to hang onto if you're the one getting washed away." They agreed and we played out the rope between us. I led off, wrapping the rope for my pack horse around the saddle horn and hanging onto the other rope with one hand. Kate came next, followed by Jim. The current was strong and extremely cold around my calves and feet, but Archie swam through it steadily, having no problems. We gained the bank on the other side and I saw that Kate and Jim were doing the same. I heaved a sigh of relief as I saw their horses gain footing on my side. They passed the rope back to me, and I felt a ton of anxiety lifted from my shoulders

Now we could move on to what we had come for. The place we were looking for first, according to what Anne had related to Jim, was a very large pine tree, struck by lightning, at the mouth of a small trail leading back to some cliffs. Raton Pass reared into the sky in front of us and we gained elevation quickly. We were expecting to follow this trail for only a few miles before reaching this first landmark. The rocky cliff faces we could see were on our left as we moved north, and that matched Jim's recollection of Anne's description. So, we concentrated our search to the west of us, checking only occasionally to the east. We took our time. Starting over and retracing our steps would be the most time consuming of all.

We took a quick break for lunch, then remounted and moved on. It was early afternoon, maybe a couple hours after crossing the Canadian, when I saw the first possible match for the landmark we were looking for. It wasn't as clear-cut as I would have hoped, but it seemed like a possibility. Twenty years could change a lot of things. Kate and Jim came up beside me, and we all got down to take a look. A huge tree had fallen across what appeared to be a faint trail leading off to the north and west. All foliage was long since gone from the tree, but it appeared to have been a pine. We began to walk the length of the tree, checking both sides of the trunk. There, maybe only ten feet up the trunk was a huge gash running upwards for about twenty feet. Only about half of the trunk was intact. What remained was wet from recent rains and almost moldy, but there were blackened areas around the edges of the gash that suggested lightning strike.

Well, I thought, the tree, though no longer standing, could certainly fit the description we had of the beginning of the trail leading back to the gold. The real question, though, was whether this faint path leading off to the north and west could really qualify as the trail we were looking for. It seemed like a fairly distinct trail for only maybe twenty or thirty yards, then narrowed down sharply and seemed to almost disappear among the thick stands of trees and underbrush.

All three of us gazed uncertainly along the path in front of us, then consulted on our next move. We agreed that it would be good to follow this path, or trail, or whatever it was, far enough to determine if it seemed likely to follow all the way through to the cliffs. We could only catch glimpses of those cliffs through the occasional breaks in the tree line. We decided it was enough of a possibility that we couldn't pass it up. We proceeded on foot, single file, after first tying up the packhorses in a clump of trees hidden from the road we had just left. We moved easily for the first twenty yards, leading the horses through the trees and proceeding with as little noise as possible. We were very aware that we had moved into an area that could be home to some small bands of Apaches.

After those first twenty or thirty yards, the path narrowed considerably. Was this a trail used by the Apaches, was it just a game trail, or had it at one time been a trail used by the Apaches and had now fallen into disuse? There were places where the saddle on Archie's back seemed to brush the trees on both sides as we passed through. Low hanging branches from the occasional juniper tree had to be pushed away from our faces. We worked our way through for a least a mile, and I think we were all getting a little doubtful and discouraged when we rounded a turn and the trail seemed to widen and become more distinct. We stopped to evaluate what we were looking at and considered our options.

We stood together and peered through the trees at where this trail might lead. It disappeared around a slight curve, maybe fifty yards ahead, and the only way to say with any certainty where it might lead would be to follow it now. We weren't prepared to do that. It was mid-afternoon already, and we estimated that it would be dark before we could reach those cliffs. Besides, our supplies were back there on the packhorses, and we would need them to carry out the gold if we found any. We agreed to return to the packhorses and the road to the Raton Pass. We would decide our next move from there.

Upon reaching the road, we looked back at the fallen pine tree and debated on the need for something to make our landmark a little clearer. In dim light, it was possible we could miss it. On the other hand, we didn't want to do anything to attract the attention of any possible bands of warriors. Or some of the riff-raff that might be passing through one the way to Cimarron, for that matter. I debated taking my ax and chopping a little gash in the tree, but the fresh blade marks could be a giveaway. We finally opted for rolling a large boulder from the side of the road to the base of the pine tree. Jim and I stood back and surveyed our handiwork and decided it was good. We were too tired to push that boulder any more, anyway.

By that time, it was late afternoon, moving on toward early evening. We decided we would camp here, but in the time we had left before dark, we would look for any other possible places we should explore before checking this one out more fully. We mounted up and moved up the road toward Raton Pass again, checking the area on our left carefully. I pulled up after about an hour, looking at another possible place in front of me. There was a lightning-struck pine tree standing at the edge of the road. Behind it was something I wasn't sure I could call a path, but there did seem to be a cleared area leading back into the trees. We walked around the tree a few times and walked a few tentative yards along the trail.

It didn't seem like as good a possibility as the first one. In any case, we were losing daylight rapidly, especially with the trees towering over us. The air had turned chilly. We decided to go back and camp for the evening. In the morning we could decide exactly how we wanted to proceed.

Murchison and Duke watched from concealment across the road. All three of them had gone into the trees over there about two hours ago, after first examining a fallen tree, for some reason.

When they'd moved on through the woods on foot, Murchison and Duke had begun to follow. Then they found the pack horses. No need to traipse through Apache country on foot. Reilly would be coming back for the pack horses. They had settled down to wait it out. Now all three had returned, and the two men were rolling a large boulder into the trees. They stopped in front of the fallen pine tree. Comprehension slowly dawned on Murchison. It was a landmark.

"What're they doing?" Duke asked him. "I dunno." No need to share information. "They seem to be interested in this area, though. Probably time to ride back and tell Moore." "You think?" Duke stared absently as Reilly and the others walked away from the boulder. "Yeah, I think they're settling in to look for something here. Better go back and get him. If you leave now and keep moving, you can see him tomorrow. I can meet you right here day after tomorrow." Duke considered that for a moment, then nodded. He waited until the three had mounted and resumed following the road toward Raton Pass, then he headed in the other direction.

Murchison watched Duke ride away, then thought about what he'd seen. He had a decision to make first—did he need to follow Reilly and the other two? He crossed the road on foot and walked back into the woods. The packhorses were still there. No need to go anywhere right now. He walked over and looked into the saddle bags. Nothing of much interest there. He went back across the road and settled into his hiding spot. These three had left in a bit of a secretive way, meeting up on the other side of Cimarron. They were heading into the mountains with packhorses. It suggested bringing something of value out of there. Gold? Perhaps.

He'd had some money once in his life. He'd robbed a bank in El Paso. Killed the bank owner when the man had hesitated to open the safe. That didn't bother him. He'd gotten away with enough money to live high on the hog for a while in California and he'd like to do it again. He thought about what he would do if these three came out with money before Duke and Moore got here. There were two of them plus the girl, but he could shoot from concealment. Then he might have to deal with Moore afterwards. He'd have to think about that. Duke, he wasn't worried about.

Duke kicked his horse into a run and kept him at it. Duke wanted to cross the Canadian tonight and get to Cimarron tomorrow. He wasn't quite sure what was happening, but it seemed like there could be some money in it and he didn't want Murchison to be there by himself if there was money. A couple hours of hard riding, and the Canadian River came into sight. There was just enough light left to get across.

Kyle Moore sat in the saloon, his anger growing by the minute. He'd made it clear they needed to report back and he should have heard by now. He pulled his watch from his pocket for the fifth or sixth time in the last hour and checked it again, mumbling under his breath as he shoved it back in his pocket. As he swung around to order another whiskey, he saw the old barkeeper watching him. He forced a calmer expression, waved his glass slowly, and sat back in the chair as he waited for his refill. He reproached himself mentally for letting his anger show. He knew from experience that the small mistakes could arouse suspicion and foul up the best planned jobs. He'd spent a few years as a guest in the Yuma territorial prison that would always remind him of that. That was about twelve years ago. He wasn't actually sure he could survive that heat again if he had to go back.

Forcing a calmness he didn't feel, he reviewed the possible things that might have happened and what he should do if somebody didn't show up soon. It was possible they'd lost Reilly somewhere on the trail and were too scared to come back and tell him about it. If so, they were halfway to Texas by now and there was nothing he could do about it. It was possible they'd figured out what Reilly's trip was about and had decided to cut him out and take the money (assuming there was some money) for themselves. And it was possible they were slow in getting back to him. He decided he would wait one more day.

Another forty-five minutes passed, and he had a growing conviction that the old barkeep was watching him. He'd about decided to go back to the bench in front of his hotel when the batwing doors opened and Duke came in. He walked over and took a seat. He looked and smelled like he'd made a hard ride to get here. Moore ordered a whiskey for him. Ordinarily he was too tight-fisted to buy another man a drink, but he needed all the information he could get from Duke. He leaned in expectantly.

Duke chugged the whiskey, gulped a glass of water and waved for another whiskey. Moore masked his impatience and waited for Duke to talk. After the second whiskey, Duke began: "We trailed him for the better part of two days…" "Did he see you?" Duke interrupted. "No. We stayed out of sight. They took the road for Raton Pass and Trinidad, but stopped before they got to either. Crossed the Canadian River and went just a few miles, then they stopped and seemed like they were looking around for something." That one got Moore's attention. "What do you mean?"

Duke described how the party had stopped at a point of the road to look at a fallen tree, then followed a trail of some kind for a couple hours. Moore interrupted: "You followed?" "No, they left their packhorses so Murchison decided we should just wait till they came back." Moore sat back and considered that one. "Did you look at the pack horses?" Duke looked for another whiskey, but Moore wasn't offering any more. "Yeah we took a look. Food mostly." "No mining stuff – picks, shovels, mesh...?" Moore asked. "Nah," Duke replied, "nothing like that." He waited to see if he was going to get interrupted again. Moore just waved his hand impatiently.

Duke went on to describe how they came back from exploring the trail, then rolled a big rock in front of the pine tree. "Landmark," Moore mumbled. Duke stopped, stared at him and mentioned that Reilly and his friends had continued down the road to Raton Pass just before Duke had left to return here. He emphasized that Murchison was still watching them, and wanted to meet up at the pine tree turnoff when Duke and Moore could get there.

Moore sat back to consider what this meant. Duke was watching him intently, which annoyed him tremendously. He fumbled in his pocket for a couple coins, which he dropped on the table. "Here, get yourself a meal. Maybe a bath too. Be ready to leave in one hour." Duke pocketed the coins and left.

Moore, welcoming the absence of Duke, leaned back in his chair, wheels turning. They had taken packhorses with them, but had stopped off a little short of the mountains. Whatever supplies they were putting on the packhorses weren't the normal things you'd get in town for ranch needs. They didn't have any mining equipment, so they weren't looking for gold... or were they? A secret trip to someplace in the mountains, with something heavy they were bringing out. Maybe they were retrieving something valuable. Gold was the only thing that came to mind. He tossed some more coins on the table, pushed back his chair so suddenly he had to grab it so it wouldn't tip over, and hurried out. He didn't notice how interested the old barkeeper was now.

Sam dried his hands on a towel behind the bar and called his nephew over. "Lenny," he said, I think I'm going to take that hunting trip after all." His nephew gave him a surprised look. "Kinda sudden, huh?" Sam ignored the question as he started to walk toward the storeroom. "Can you hold this place together for a few days? You know what to do, right?" Lenny nodded. "You can get your brother Mike to help if it gets too busy in the evenings. He can probably spare a few hours from watching the ranch." He tossed his apron over his shoulder onto the bar. "Good. Gotta go."

Sam grabbed his guns, ammunition, food, and a couple blankets from the storeroom. It took him a couple trips to put them all on the back porch. He then set out at a trot toward the livery stable, where he kept his horse. His bruised ribs reminded him of his recent adventures so he slowed down to a fast walk. He led his horse out of the stable and around to the back door of the saloon. He saddled up the horse and loaded his gear. There wasn't much food, so he added a fishing line in case he needed a couple extra meals. Then he walked through the saloon to the front porch and pretended to sweep some more. The porch hadn't been this clean in years.

He didn't have to keep up the façade for very long. Down the street, he could see the man from the bar with his usual two tied down guns carrying some gear out of the hotel and loading it on his horse. Within another fifteen minutes the other man who'd been talking to him came down the street, leading his horse. Sam kept his head down as the man passed. They met up in front of the hotel and rode out of town together. Sam waited ten minutes, mounted his horse and began to follow slowly.

Chapter Ten

Unwelcome Visitors

In the morning, we were glad for the extra blanket or two we had packed. Kate and I had snuggled up next to each other for warmth. Jim was on his own—I'm not sure what he did but I didn't notice any frostbite. We all had a little incentive to get this done and head on home with the prize.

At first blush, we had two possible avenues to follow, but after a little thought, we realized we actually had three. We could follow the trail we were currently camped beside, with the fallen pine tree marking the way, we could follow the one down the road we had scouted briefly yesterday evening, or we could first follow the road to Raton Pass for a couple more miles or so to eliminate the possibility of a third option. If there were something else that looked better than either of the first two, we didn't want to overlook it. After some discussion, we opted for the third choice. Following either of the first two trails was liable to be time consuming, and we needed to be sure there wasn't a better possibility first.

Resuming the trail toward Raton Pass brought more altitude quickly. We kept our collars turned up against the cold wind and kept a sharp watch for scarred or fallen trees near a trail on our left. We came to the one we'd seen the previous evening and looked it over again briefly in the morning light. We agreed that the first one with the fallen pine tree was still more promising. We turned back into the road to Raton and stayed with it until the sun was high and directly overhead. We broke for lunch and decided we had followed the road to Raton far enough. We would go back and follow the first trail to see where it might lead.

We arrived back at the spot where we'd left the packhorses and first had to make a decision on the supplies. We knew we could bury some of the food supplies or sling them over a tree limb, but we might need them. We'd be consuming them as we went, so hopefully the horses could carry any gold we found along with supplies.

We followed the trail as we had the day before, well aware with each hour that passed we were deeper into possible Apache hunting grounds. We followed as the trail alternately widened and narrowed, drawing closer to the cliffs and rocky faces in front of us. We came to our first decision point around the middle of the afternoon. For the first time, we weren't entirely sure which way the trail led. We had come to a fork in the road, with only a faint trace of a trail proceeding to our right. The one to the left was better defined, but not by much. We sat our horses and evaluated what we could see in each direction, with no good clues about which fork to take. Jim eventually volunteered to take the path on the right for a few hundred yards while we waited for word on what he found.

Kate and I remained at the fork in the trail, talking in low tones while we could hear the faint sounds of Jim's horse proceeding down the path to the right. After a few minutes our talk subsided and we could no longer hear Jim. We waited silently for him to return. Suddenly there was a shot, followed by Jim's voice shouting: "Chance! Kate! Sam! Mike!" His shouts were immediately followed by another gunshot. We turned the packhorses loose and I slapped Archie and urged him down the trail, shouting at Kate to stay close behind me. Staying quiet was no longer an issue. I fired a couple shots into the air and Kate did the same, hoping to convince whoever Jim was battling that a lot of help was on the way. He had clearly shouted extra names to accomplish just that.

After a quick turn in the trail, we burst into a small clearing. I could hear the noise of a few horses dashing in the other direction, but paid no attention to that for the moment. An Apache lay on his back in the middle of the clearing. The size and location of the wound in his chest told me in an instant that he didn't merit any further attention. My eyes swung rapidly about the clearing and after a moment I could see Jim slumped against a tree at the edge of the trees. There was blood trickling down the side of his head. I swung down, pistol in hand, and sprinted to him. I knelt and took a quick glance at the wound on his head. A bullet had plowed a furrow through the hairline near the temple and he was clearly stunned. I began to tear my bandana from around my neck to put pressure on the wound. Behind me I heard Kate say, "I have bandages and water!" Her footsteps receded and it didn't dawn on me in the moment that she had gone back to her packhorse to get them.

I stood up, grabbed my canteen from Archie and held it up for Jim to take a drink. I poured most of the rest of the water over the wound and applied slight pressure with the bandana. I propped Jim up against the tree next to him and he seemed to revive a bit. I sat back with some relief and saw a little color returning to his face. He mumbled a few words I couldn't hear, so I leaned closer. He mumbled again, but this time I caught the words. "Where's Kate?" I stood and spun around, searching the clearing. She wasn't there. I pulled Jim a little deeper into the woods, leaned him against a pine tree, took the revolver from where it lay in the ground next to him, and put it into his hands. He nodded and mumbled again, this time with a little more force behind the words. "Go get her."

I took Archie back down the trail as fast as the terrain would allow, branches tearing my shirt sleeves and slapping against my face as I hunched over Archie's neck. Finally, I could see both packhorses tethered where we had left them. I burst into the small clearing at the fork in the road and I swung around, searching the trees and the ground around the clearing. My worst fears had been realized. Kate was gone.

I jumped from Archie's back, pistol in my hand though I had no memory of drawing it. I circled the area again and again, seeing mostly the tracks of our shod horses. I took a few steps up the fork of the trail we'd not yet explored, finally getting down on my knees to examine the ground. There were a lot of leaves and twigs on the ground, concealing to a large degree any tracks I could find, but I thought I could see a mixture of tracks for both a shod horse and an unshod pony. I straightened up and took another look around, when something else caught my eye at a turn in the trail up ahead. It was a small twig with a circle of bark removed from the middle.

Murchison had stayed with the packhorses that morning. When the three had returned from a trip up the Raton Pass road, he'd trailed them as they took the packhorses and followed the trail they had explored yesterday. Past the fallen pine tree and along the trail, he had stayed with them, hoping that whatever they were looking for would be found before Duke returned with Kyle Moore. When they came to the fork in the road, he'd hidden himself quietly in the trees while the older man explored the fork to the right in the trail.

Gunshots had sounded and he saw Reilly and the girl disappear along the fork to the right. He'd kept his head down even further. Minutes later the girl had returned. He'd witnessed a single Apache warrior materialize from the woods in front of him. The brave had attacked and subdued the girl, tied her up and tied her to her horse. In a matter of only a few minutes they had disappeared along the other fork in the trail. Still, he had remained hidden where he was.

Reilly had returned and scouted the ground around the area. Murchison was pretty sure that Reilly had figured out what had happened. The older man was nowhere in sight. Reilly, to his surprise, went back up the fork to the right and disappeared. Now, Murchison had a decision to make. He knew that whatever they had been looking for didn't matter at this point. They'd be looking for the girl, who had been taken by the Apaches. This changed everything. The money he'd hoped for wasn't in the picture. A running fight with Apaches was in the picture instead. This, Murchison reasoned, wasn't his fight. He decided he would return to the meeting point by the pine tree on the Raton Pass road and tell Moore what he knew tomorrow.

I raced back to where I'd left Jim as quickly as the path would allow. I swung down in the clearing and ran to where I'd left him. He was still sitting, propped up against the tree, gun in hand. He seemed a little stronger, but told me he still felt dizzy and his head hurt pretty badly. He hadn't tried getting up from where he was. I broke the news to him they had taken Kate and saw the fear and anger flash across his face. He tried to rise, but slumped back against the tree. I had an impossible dilemma; I couldn't leave him here alone, but I had to go after Kate immediately. Jim solved it for me.

"Tie me in the saddle," he said. "If you tie me on my horse, I'll hold on. "Let's go after her now." He held on to me as I helped him rise and climb on to his horse. I passed a rope around his waist and under the horse, and another around his legs to secure him to the saddle. I glanced at his hands, which were gripping the saddle horns. "I can hold on," he said. "I don't need my hands tied." I nodded, passed rope between the horses and led him back down the trail to the clearing where Kate had been taken.

We stopped long enough to tie the packhorses behind Jim's horse, then proceeded single file down the left-hand fork of the trail. I picked up the twig Kate had whittled and showed it to him, explaining the conversation Kate and I had on the way out. He nodded, the movement costing him a grimace of pain. We proceeded down the trail, keeping an eye out for any other markers, as well as any place they had left the trail. Speed was of the essence, so we had to assume they had followed the trail unless we saw hoofprints leaving it.

Kate had neither seen nor heard him coming. She had been shocked and scared at seeing her father laying on the ground and bleeding. Coming back for bandages and water had been pure instinct. She reproached herself a little for not remembering the dangerous situation they were in, but nothing could be done about that now. She could only concentrate on the situation she had at hand.

The brave had come on her silently and he was extremely strong. She was on the ground before she knew it, her weapons out of reach. He'd dragged her toward the packhorses and reached for some rope to tie her, and she'd had the presence of mind to put her hands in front of her. The twigs remained in her pocket and she was able to reach them. It was a small thing, but it was something. He had tied her on the horse, with her hands tied to the saddle horn. She could still reach the inner pocket of her jacket by leaning forward. He had tied her bandana around her mouth to silence any calls for help.

After looking through the packs on the saddle horses and briefly evaluating the animals themselves, he'd left them there, probably because he felt the need to travel fast and light. He led her horse by holding a rope he had tied around the horse's neck. He led the way down the left fork of the trail. Kate leaned forward and pulled a twig from the inner pocket. She waited until he looked forward down the trail, then tossed the twig quickly to the side of the path. They continued down the trail, and she decided she would only risk marking the path again if they turned off this trail or came to another fork in the road.

Her thoughts turned toward her father and Chance. Her dad had been stunned and in pain, but it may have been only a graze wound along the scalp. That would hurt him, as it clearly had, but it might not be serious. She thought about Chance. He would look after her father, and she knew he wouldn't stop coming after her as long as he had breath to pursue. She had to look for every opportunity to help him. She was so lost in her thoughts she almost didn't notice a faint game trail branching off to the right. She reached in her pocket and tossed another twig on the main trail as they continued. Her gaze swung back to the narrow game trail they had passed. It appeared to lead straight back to the cliffs. It could have been what they were looking for.

Now she could hear the sound of hoofbeats coming up from the rear. Her heart leaped at the thought it was Chance, then sunk when she realized it was the sound of several horses. The brave in front of her swung around, bow and arrow at the ready. He lowered the bow when three Apaches braves rounded the bend in the trail and came up to them. The new arrivals stared at her and traded several comments back and forth with her captor. After a brief argument, one fell alongside her captor in front and the other two followed. She hoped they didn't make any turns off the trail now. Marking the trail was probably too dangerous.

Another hour found them emerging into a small clearing surrounded by some rocky outcroppings and occasional pine trees. She was surprised to see another band of Apaches who appeared to be breaking camp and moving on. This didn't appear to be a war party. She counted ten braves, three squaws and two small children, probably no older than six or seven. They two groups seemed to know each other. They conversed briefly, then the larger party moved off to the north. She noticed one of the squaws seemed to be watched or guarded. She was on the far side of the group. Kate found herself staring, then looking away. This squaw was dressed in Apache clothing and her hair was worn in a fashion no different than the other two, but her skin was noticeably lighter. As they moved away, the two other squaws moved up to place themselves between Kate and the third squaw. One of the braves rode up alongside them to further block her view. Kate looked down at the ground to mask her curiosity. Was that another white captive with this group? Whoever it was, they gave her a significant amount of freedom, but didn't seem to trust her entirely.

She was distracted from any further thoughts on the subject as her captors began setting up a camp. They quickly erected four small teepees from some materials left behind by the other group and yanked her roughly from her horse, pushing her inside one of the teepees and out of sight. The warrior who had captured her back at the fork in the trail took up a guard position outside the tent. She had no way to protect herself, and she couldn't imagine she would go to sleep. It was going to be a long night.

Jim and I were following along the trail as quickly as we could. An assessment of the tracks we could see showed us only two horses. It stood to reason that one brave had been following behind the others and had found Kate when she returned to the fork in the trail. We needed to stay close behind them, but we had to be careful about running into the other warriors. Jim thought there were three more, besides the one he had killed. He had noticed only one rifle among them. The others were armed only with bows and arrows, and of course, tomahawks. The three warriors attacking Jim had dispersed when they heard the sound of gunfire as Kate and I had come down the trail toward them. They had probably done so, Jim thought, because they didn't know how many they would be facing.

We stopped pretty often. In part, I wanted Jim to gain more strength. He sipped water each time we stopped, his color looked better and he told me the headache was beginning to subside. The other reason we stopped was because we knew there were three warriors unaccounted for out there. We came to a small fork in the trail, with a game trail leading off toward the north. It appeared to head into some cliffs and rocky faces. We dismounted and began looking for tracks in either direction. In a moment, I spotted another marker twig, cast down at the side of the main trail leading left. I scooped it up and turned to show Jim when I heard the sound of hoofbeats approaching from behind us. We quickly grabbed the reins of our horses and pulled up the game trail a short way before taking cover in the trees at the side of the trail. We were none too soon as three Apache warriors came down the trail in front of us, pausing only briefly before proceeding down the main trail to the left.

We gave them a half hour or so before following. We assumed they were going to meet up with the other warrior and Kate, but we didn't want to catch up to them too soon. Luckily, the tracks of five horses were easier to follow than two, and we proceeded at a steady pace. The trail began to climb a little in elevation and the sun began casting lengthening shadows as afternoon turned to evening. We dismounted and proceeded on foot. They may be making camp for the night soon. As the trail climbed higher and the cover from the trees began to thin out, we saw what we were looking for. They had made camp in a small clearing at the foot of some rocky outcroppings overlooking the clearing. We turned and walked the horses back several hundred yards, then tethered them to a tree. We proceeded back on foot, bending over to stay low, then crawling the last hundred yards or so to peer out from atop one of the outcroppings. I could see them leading Kate toward the fire where they had prepared some food. Her hands were tied, but they were removing a bandana they'd used as a gag to silence her. I saw with relief that she appeared to be unharmed.

Chapter Eleven

Now or Never

We kept our heads down as we watched the clearing from the promontory where we lay concealed. There were just the four warriors plus Kate, which is what we had expected. They led Kate to the campfire and pushed her down to the ground on the other side of it. She sat facing our position. One of the four gathered the horses and led them across toward the other side of the clearing, no doubt intending to secure them in the trees for the night. One returned to one of the teepees and disappeared inside. That left two, one tending the fire and the other roasting some kind of meat. I waited for my chance and hoped for a little luck.

My chance came when both Apaches around the campfire turned their backs to me. A quick glance told me the third was still in the teepee and the fourth in the trees on the other side of the clearing. I scrambled to my feet and sky lined myself against the setting sun, which was disappearing in the west directly behind me. As I'd hoped, the movement caught her eye. She glanced up, shielded her eyes and did a quick double take, then looked back down at the ground. I hoped she had recognized me. She was tied up, but might still find a way to help when we came for her. Jim and I then crawled down and away from our position, returning to the horses. We had some planning to do before daybreak.

Kate's heart leaped when she saw Chance outline himself against the sky. She immediately dropped her gaze and stared at the ground, hoping she hadn't given him away. She cast a sidelong glance at the two by the fire, who only went about doing what they had before. That left the other two, but she knew Chance would have taken them into account before standing up. They brought some kind of charred meat from the fire and pushed it into her hands, then dropped a skin of some kind next to her. She assumed it was water. The meat had a pungent smell and was very tough, but she chewed and swallowed it anyway. She might need all her strength before morning. She managed to pick up the animal skin with her bound hands and drank some water.

Kate waited while the other two braves came back and began eating. She noticed they all appeared to ignore her, but she had the feeling they would be aware of any moves she made. Getting her hands untied was her top priority, but the rope was securely bound and cutting it would be her only hope. She surveyed the ground around her as casually as she could, but there were no rocks in the area within reach at all, let alone a rock with sharp edges. She was propped up against something hard and sharp behind her, but now it was a disadvantage to have her hands tied in front. They would be able to see anything she did. The four talked among themselves as they ate, arguing briefly at times. She decided they were probably making plans for tomorrow in particular, and what they were going to do with her in general. It wasn't a comforting thought.

Eventually one of them, her original captor, pulled her to her feet roughly and half-dragged her back across the clearing to the teepee where she'd been kept earlier. He opened the flap and pushed her inside, where she tripped and fell, breaking her fall with her bound hands. She pushed herself back up to her knees, and while there was still a little daylight left, searched the ground around her for anything sharp enough to cut the rope. There was nothing. She sighed in disappointment and sank back to her knees. She still needed a plan of some kind.

When would they come for her? Dawn, was her best guess. They couldn't accomplish much in the dark, and the moon would give only a sliver of light tonight, as it had last night. Just a little dawn light would give them enough to move in while still preserving some concealment. What could she do to help? Only one thing came to mind: they had removed her gag. Perhaps she could create something of a distraction if needed, or maybe give a warning to Chance if that's what the situation called for. She decided to see if she could get any sleep at all. She knew she would be awake well before dawn. A quick glance through the flap told her the same brave was on duty outside. She curled up on the ground to see if she could nap a little.

Murchison could hear them coming from his hideout near the fallen pine tree. Clearly, they weren't making any effort to remain quiet. He felt the familiar contempt he'd been feeling for the other two since the beginning. If there was a way to eliminate those two and still recover whatever Reilly was searching for, he'd be working on that plan in a hurry. He emerged cautiously from his place of concealment, checked to make sure that Reilly and the other two hadn't returned, then stepped out into the road to flag down Moore and Duke. He led them back to the hideout and turned to give Moore the explanation he knew would be demanded.

Moore beat him to it. "Where are they?" he demanded. "I don't know," Murchison answered. He paused deliberately just to let Moore get up a full head of steam. Moore's face took on a slight shade of purple. "You don't..." he began. Murchison cut him off. "Injuns took the girl." He had the satisfaction of watching his statement shut down Moore's tirade before it could really get started. Moore paused, one fist in the air, spluttering as he searched for his next words. Finally, he just stopped and stared at Murchison, visually demanding an explanation.

"I followed them down that trail right over there. Starts on the other side of that pine tree laying on the ground." He pointed. Moore swung to take a look, then swung back to lock in on Murchison. Duke merely looked on curiously. His attitude seemed to say he'd finished his job when he got Moore back to the rendezvous. Moore waved his hand impatiently for more. "They took the packhorses this time," Murchison continued, "so I followed. They didn't seem to be looking for anything, just following that trail. They came to a fork in the road, so I hid back in the trees and waited. One of them, the older guy, went off to explore one fork while Reilly and girl waited. There were gunshots, so Reilly and the girl took off after the old guy. After a while the girl came back by herself and a brave grabbed her." "Just one?" Moore interrupted. Murchison nodded. "Just one. Anyway, after a while, Reilly and the old guy came back. The old guy was bleeding a little and looked like he was tied in the saddle. They looked around for a sign, then went down the other fork in the road, where the Injun took the girl. I came back here."

Moore erupted again. "You came back here?" he shouted. He was incensed. "What good are you doing here?" Murchison looked at him and for the first time Moore sensed the intense dislike, maybe even hatred Murchison had for him. It crossed his mind that Murchison might draw on him, and he casually moved his hand toward his right hand gun. He was quite sure he could take Murchison. It just wasn't time yet. The movement wasn't lost on Murchison, who just watched and waited. "Go on," said Moore in a calmer tone.

"I had to be here to meet you, didn't I?" demanded Murchison, one eye still on Moore's right hand gun. "So, I came back. Besides, after hearing several gunshots, I'm pretty sure it wasn't just one Apache that took the girl. I agreed to follow Reilly and figure out what he's lookin' for. I'll do that. I ain't going to lose my scalp in an Injun fight that don't concern me." He stared defiantly at Moore, who swallowed his anger and nodded. "OK," he said. The calm tone he used cost him dearly, considering how much he wanted to throttle Murchison. "We'll follow them now. All three of us. If the Apaches kill them, we're done. If they kill the Apaches and get the girl back, we're back in business. We have no part of the Indian fight. Agreed?" He looked at both men, who both nodded. Moore turned and started leading his horse out toward the fallen pine tree.

Sam waited under the cover of the pines and junipers, staring up ahead to where he'd seen the third man flag down the two men he'd been following. It had been ridiculously easy to trail them so far. They appeared to have no concern that someone might be on their trail. Sam's lips curled up a little at the irony of that one. Well, maybe he could surprise them a little before this was done. He took a swig of water from his canteen and continued watching. They had made camp short of the Canadian River last night, so he had done the same. They'd made a late start this morning. Sam glanced overhead. It was midday or a little later. Movement ahead caught his eye and he looked down toward the road again. All three were emerging from the trees and appeared to be taking a trail across the road from their position.

Sam mounted up but waited, chewing a piece of jerky and washing it down with a little more water while he gave them a little time to move on ahead. Based on his experience so far, he didn't need to worry about losing them. They might as well have left a map with instructions for him. When he judged they had gone sufficiently far down the trail, he eased his horse out on to the road and cantered down to the spot where he'd last seen them. He came to a place where a fallen pine tree with a large boulder in front of it seemed to point toward a trail leading off toward the mountains. Sam eased up beside the tree and looked it over. Maybe Chance had found what he was looking for, after all. Sam turned his horse and moved down the trail, alternately checking for sign and keeping an eye out for Apaches. Come to think of it, he could keep an eye out for a trail leading to those cliffs he could see to his right. He didn't doubt that the buried gold might still be out here somewhere.

I laid alongside Jim on top of the rock ledge overlooking the Apache camp and watched as they ate and went about securing the horses and camp. They had taken Kate back to the teepee at the far edge of the field from our position, and it looked like a certainty they intended to hold her there tonight. It also looked like they would alternate on night watch—two and two. I still saw evidence of only one rifle among them, which made things considerably easier. We were outmanned but had more firepower. We conferred just as the sun began to set. It was decided that Jim would lay down covering fire from up here while I went around to the other side to pull Kate out of the teepee. Their choice of campsite had both an obvious advantage and an obvious disadvantage. It helped us considerably to have a clear field of fire from up here. It was a problem, however, for me to try to sneak up on them across the open field to get to Kate's position. Maybe it was a reflection of the kind of up-close weaponry they were used to using. I had to hope it didn't come down to that.

We agreed on basic strategy before I left to take up my position. I would rely on keeping silent for as long as I could. When the shooting started, Jim would take out the man with the rifle first. After that, he would fire at whoever had enough distance from Kate and me so as not to endanger either of us. Up-close fighting was up to me, starting with the guard on Kate's tent. I hoped I would be able to surprise him and get the jump. I knew very well how skilled they were at hand-to-hand fighting. After I had freed Kate, we would run directly toward Jim's position, allowing him to take out anyone behind us.

I began the long circling move to take me behind the teepee where they held Kate. Silence was a must, so it was about an hour later, with darkness taking over, when I finally reached my hiding place. I estimated I would have to cover about forty yards to reach the back edge of Kate's teepee. The brave guarding her was stationed outside the flap on the other side. At least I had the teepee itself to shield me from his view.

Sleep seemed to be out of the question. I laid there for the long hours of that night, mentally picking my way across that field. It was too dark now to see if there was anything to obstruct my path. Once or twice the sentinel outside the teepee made a circle around it. If he did that while I was crossing the space, that was a problem. I'd seen earlier there were no boulders or barriers to hide behind between here and there. I looked around and saw a few boulders on the other side of the teepee, but they wouldn't be of any use to me. I could only hope my timing was good.

The night passed so slowly that I was beginning to think it was my imagination when I saw a little gray light filtering across the meadow. A few more minutes and I knew that dawn was finally arriving. I began to estimate how much light Jim needed to lay down fire from his position. I gave it another five minutes and began to crawl. Daylight showed a few dry sticks and rocks I hadn't seen during my nighttime vigil. I rose to a crouching position to move forward. I might be a little more visible, but hopefully also quieter. I moved slowly and steadily, dropping occasionally to a full crouching position to survey the field. I saw no movement.

 I finally gained the friendly shelter of the back side of the teepee. I was only feet away from pulling Kate out of there. My hopes rose as I stood and pulled my Colt from the holster, turned and stepped forward to circle the teepee. When I did, my foot fell on a small dry twig sticking out from under the teepee wall. There was a small but audible crunching noise. I froze...

Kate thought she might have napped a little during the night, but that was far behind her now. She could see the growing dawn light filtering through. Her hopes of a rescue before morning began to sink. With each day, the difficulty would increase for Chance to find her. She glanced out through the flap in the teepee. Her guard seemed to be dozing. She looked toward the back wall of her shelter and caught her breath. Did she see the vague outline of a human shape creeping toward her? She concentrated and watched. After a minute or two, she was sure. There was somebody crouched outside the back of the teepee. Friend or foe was the obvious question. If it was a member of a warring faction or another tribe come to steal her away, she could wind up worse off. She dared not make any noise in case it was Chance. The figure rose and she saw the shadowy outline of a revolver. Chance! She turned to see if the guard was still sleeping. Then she heard the soft crack of a twig. The warrior in front came to his feet pulling a knife. Chance needed a distraction... she let loose a deafening scream. The Apache froze for an instant and looked in her direction.

When Kate screamed, I knew it was now or never. I rushed around the teepee in time to see the Apache warrior turning to me and setting his feet. In the gray light I could see the dull gleam of a knife blade rising toward me in a vicious uppercut. I swung my revolver as hard as I could, slamming the barrel across his forehead. He went down like a stone, knife falling at his feet. I snatched it up and plunged into the teepee, not certain if Kate was alone. To my immense relief, she was. I saw her rising to meet me, then heard the sound of a rifle shot. A bullet ripped through, too close for comfort. I tackled Kate and lay on top of her. Another shot passed through both walls of the teepee just above us. Then a third shot sounded and a fourth, both coming from farther away. Was it just covering fire, or had Jim had a clear shot at him? I risked a glance out the flap and saw a warrior down across the field. The one I'd hammered with my revolver lay at my feet and he wasn't moving.

There were two of them left out there. No time to lose. I used the Apache's knife to sever the ropes around Kate's wrists. I pulled her to her feet and we sprinted away from the teepee, headed directly toward Jim's covering position. From the corner of my eye I could see another brave coming from where they'd sheltered the horses. He had a bit of cover from some boulders over there, and he dashed from one to the next. He paused behind one, then rushed for the next when the rifle sounded again and he went down. I didn't know where the fourth one was, but we kept running and I kept my revolver handy. As we approached a spot near the edge of the field a wraith-like figure came up from behind a sizeable boulder, tomahawk in the air. I shot him point blank in the chest, and suddenly it was over.

Kate and I scrambled up the rock face until we reached Jim's position, then we collapsed into each other's arms. I could hear Kate whispering, "I knew you'd come," over and over. I was speechless with relief. The possibility of losing her had been unthinkable. Jim came over to wrap his arms around both of us. I'm not sure how much time passed. It was one of those moments you don't forget in a lifetime. Finally, I moved over to where the horses were tethered. They hadn't unsaddled Kate's horse. I grabbed his reins, scattered the Indian ponies and led him back over. We needed some distance from this place, just in case these four had any friends around.

Chapter Twelve

A Remarkable Discovery

Moore was awakened by the sound of gunfire, and it was uncomfortably close. He shifted in his blankets and squinted out, trying to estimate the time by the amount of gray light filtering through the trees. Judging it to be not much past daybreak, he threw his blankets off and struggled to his feet, picking up the gun belt and buckling that on first. He stooped to tie down the holster string around each leg, then half-drew each revolver before settling it back into the holster. It was his morning routine. He looked around and saw Murchison stirring. Duke was still sound asleep, and Moore aimed a kick into the blankets to get him moving. Duke burst out of the blankets with an angry stare which Moore returned. Duke shrugged and pulled himself to his feet. Moore reflected that they were held together only by their common lust for money, and that bond was wearing thin. It was something to keep in mind.

The sound of the gunfire seemed to fade almost as soon as it started, and now the dawn was quiet. Murchison kicked the coals from the previous evening's fire and blew on them enough to restore a small flame. They heated what was left of the previous evening's meal and made do with that for breakfast, ears tuned to any sounds they could pick up. It was likely that Reilly and the old man had tried to rescue the girl. Their trip depended on who won that contest.

They stood to gain almost nothing by moving forward to investigate right now. If Reilly had surprised the Apaches and rescued the girl, there was probably a fifty-fifty chance they would return in this direction. If the Apaches had won this morning's encounter, they stood an excellent chance of running into a victorious war party if they moved forward. Moore squelched all suggestions about moving out. He was determined to hold this position until at least mid-afternoon. If Reilly had won out and moved in the opposite direction, following was a dicey proposition at best. He would cross that bridge only if he had to.

Mid-afternoon sun was filtering through the trees when the faint sound of voices and horse hooves began to reach them. Moore had dozed off, seated and propped up against a pine tree. Murchison tossed a pine cone to get his attention. They all laid flat in the underbrush and focused attention on the trail cutting through the woods about forty yards away. Eventually they were rewarded with the sight they'd hoped to see. Reilly, the girl and the old man rode past, leading the packhorses. Signaling the others to remain, Moore gathered his horse's reins and shadowed them, picking his way through the trees and watching the path they were taking. His intuition proved right. At the juncture of the path with a small game trail leading off toward the rocky faces and cliffs, they bore left and headed toward the cliffs. After going only a few hundred yards, they stopped, gathered and began to talk. The discussion went on for several minutes. Moore frowned in confusion. What was so important to discuss at this point?

Sam heard the gunfire as he lay in his blankets in the early gray light. The shots sounded like they'd been fired from a position not far away. He'd heard both rifle fire and a pistol shot, unless he missed his guess. The pistol shot most likely would have come from Chance or Jim. He wasn't so sure about the rifle shots. He sat up, hunched over in his blankets, while he considered what to do. It was very unlikely he could get there in time to help Chance, if that's who was involved in this. The group of three he was trailing had apparently decided not to move. Maintaining his position and the element of surprise seemed like the best thing to do. Sam chewed on a cold biscuit while staring off toward the west. Had Chance and the Randolphs run into a war party?

Putting in some distance from the scene of this morning's raid seemed more important than anything. We'd stopped only for a few minute's discussion. Each of us had seen the small trail leading toward the cliffs while we were coming in the opposite direction, and that was our destination. Kate had assured her father and me that she was unhurt. With those things established, no one was of a mind to stop until we'd reached that trail. I rode point with a packhorse trailing behind me. When the trail straightened enough, I would glance back to reassure myself that Kate was still behind me. She smiled and nodded each time, so we kept going, with Jim following in the rear. We put in a steady, watchful ride of maybe two hours when I saw the game trail leading off to the north. I pulled Archie to the left and followed it for just a short distance before dismounting and joining the others.

We found a log laying alongside the trail, seated ourselves on it and had a small meal while Kate filled us in on her capture. She mentioned encountering another group of Indians, but said they didn't appear to be a war party and had moved on in the other direction, which gave us some comfort. Jim and I compared notes on the trail we were currently following, with some enthusiasm that this might be the path Gibson had followed before burying that money. None of us were much of a mind to search other trails if this one didn't pan out. Kate remained a little withdrawn and quiet during the discussion, but I put it down to what she'd been through during this last day. When we rose to remount and continue toward the cliffs, she put out a restraining hand on our arms and asked us both to sit back down. I knelt beside her and searched her face as she struggled to gather her thoughts.

"We met another party of Apaches before camping last night," she began. I nodded. She had told us this before. "Right," I said. "Not a war party. Maybe fifteen or sixteen, but with three squaws and a couple children. You told us about it. They rode the other way." Kate chewed her lip absentmindedly and nodded in agreement. "Right. There was a group of three squaws, but one was treated differently. Trusted a little but not entirely." That was an odd description. I glanced over at Jim. His face registered as much confusion as mine probably did. We waited, but Kate had fallen silent. I reached for her hand. "What are you trying to tell us?" "I think," she said, "that the third squaw might have been another white captive. Maybe someone who has been with them for a long time but isn't entirely one of them."

Her words left us all completely silent as we tried to process them. Jim cleared his throat, but wound up saying nothing, staring at the ground in front of him. Finally, I gave it a try. "How sure are you it's a white woman?" Kate shook her head miserably. "Not sure at all. I'm not even sure I should have brought it up, but it was bothering me because..." "Because of your mother." Jim finished the thought. Kate nodded silently. I sat back down on the log, and each of us was lost in thought for a while. Finally, I realized that I was the one with no personal stake here. Kate and Jim needed to make this decision. I waited, already mentally resolved to follow through on whatever they decided.

Jim squatted on his heels next to his daughter, gathering his thoughts. "What do you want to do, Kate?" She shook her head. "I don't really know what we can do. The chance they have Mom after all these years... I can't believe it's her. I couldn't get a good look at her or get any idea how old she is. She just didn't seem to be entirely trusted. She was dressed like the others, but seemed a little lighter skinned. That's all I could see." Jim looked back in the direction we had come. "They went off to the north, you said, probably back into the Sangre de Cristo Mountains. There are a number of places they might camp up in there. Probably several war parties in the area, but…"

Kate shook her head and stood up. "There's nothing we can do. There's almost no chance it's her and we probably can't even find them anyway. Let's go on." Jim was still looking toward the mountains to the north, but finally began to nod his head in agreement. "I don't know what else we can do," he finally managed in an undertone. "Chance?" "It's your call," I told them. "Whatever you decide, I'm with you." They both turned and started for the horses, mounting up and heading toward the caves and rock faces in front of us.

Sam watched from his perch among the trees and underbrush as Chance Reilly and the Randolphs passed along the trail. In between, he could see the three drifters from the saloon, also watching as Reilly and the Randolphs passed. Clearly, they had some idea there was a search underway for something valuable, and they intended to steal the valuables when found. That much was obvious. It was the unknowns that gave Sam pause and had him thinking this through yet again. His friends had gone past this spot and returned and gunfire had sounded off in the west while they were over there. That would imply they'd had a run-in with other bandits or the Apaches. Whichever it was, they seemed to have survived it in good shape.

Sam's other dilemma had to do with the fact that his presence was unknown to Chance and the Randolphs. If he could find a way to join up with them, would that be better than remaining a surprise to everyone? His gut instincts told him to remain hidden. When he made his presence known, it would be a good surprise for his friends. It would be an unpleasant surprise for the three would-be robbers. He decided to keep it that way. When the Randolphs headed for their horses, Sam eased back from his hideout and prepared to follow.

I urged Archie forward a little as we moved toward the rock faces, passing Kate on my way to talk to Jim. Obviously we'd made quite a bit of noise this morning when we went in for Kate, and it wasn't unreasonable to think we'd gone unnoticed by any other Apache war parties or hunting parties that were out there. I came alongside Jim to ask his opinion. He nodded and glanced forward as he took in my question, probably estimating how much time we'd need to get to the cliffs and caves up ahead.

"If there's another war party around, they'd have heard us, of course," he answered. "But things are a little different than they were twenty or thirty years ago. They seem to have only small bands of warriors, maybe about the size we ran into. They know they can't afford to run into the army. Even a pretty small cavalry troop is probably more trouble than they can handle. They didn't hesitate to attack a group as small as ours, but another war party out there wouldn't necessarily know that's what they're dealing with. I guess what I'm saying is, if they're out there and they heard us, they might come looking or they might not." He looked ahead toward the cliffs again. "I'll feel a little better in a couple hours when we can get some protection at our backs."

That made sense to me. I dropped back to the rear of our procession, thinking now about what we knew as far as where the gold might be buried. Gibson had told Anne Randolph he'd carved a crescent moon symbol to the right of a cave entrance after burying the gold inside. When we'd started out that had seemed like the easiest landmark we would be looking for. Now, looking up at the cliff faces, I wasn't so sure. There might be half a dozen caves near the end of this trail, and who knows how deeply Gibson would have etched that symbol, what with a dozen Apache warriors coming after him? Well... we had come this far. We would give it a good thorough search.

Mid-afternoon brought us to the end of the trail we had followed. We had now reached the cliffs and rocky faces at the southern edge of the Sangre de Cristo Mountains. There'd been a time or two I thought I'd heard some movement in the underbrush behind me, but I was probably just a little jumpy after this morning's adventure. Each time I had reined Archie around and searched visually, seeing nothing each time. I dismounted with the others and studied the area we'd come to. The rock face was accessible for probably a couple hundred yards in either direction. There might be four or five cave entrances along the rock face we were looking at. Three seemed fairly accessible if we could scramble up the face a little way. Two more looked like a lot of work would be involved to scale to the entrance. We could leave those for last.

Safety was at the top of the list for all of us. The cave closest to the end of the trail was also the most accessible. The slope was easy and gradual, and a quick inspection told us it was roomy enough inside to bring in the horses. There was no entrance or exit at the rear, but air was escaping through an area at the back and toward the top of the cave. We brought the horses in with only a minimum of tugging and encouragement. The cave mouth wasn't high enough up to command a wide field of fire, but trees and underbrush largely obscured the approach anyway, with an open area only thirty yards or so deep in front of the entrance. We would take shifts on guard duty at night. A quick examination of the walls at the entrance showed no scratching or carving marks of any kind. The interior also showed no evidence of digging or burial of anything.

We could cover the most ground by splitting up and searching, but we'd had near-disaster when we split up yesterday. There was time to explore maybe one cave before setting up camp for the evening. We opted to search the cave on the left together. The wall at the right front showed a few circular marks. It was questionable whether or not they were man-made, but twenty years had gone by. We chose to be thorough and check it out. This one had been used for shelter at some point in the past. There were discarded rags here and there. A natural shelf toward the back held a dull pick and some wire mesh. Both suggested a miner's tools. The cave had a number of twists to it, which we explored to the very back wall. There was no evidence of anything buried, and we found no rock piles or diggings of any size.

We had agreed to stop after one cave and set up for tonight's camp. We returned to our original cave. Jim began pulling cooking pots and blankets from the packs, after which he led the horses back out to graze until dark. Kate started a cooking fire for dinner. I went out to find as much fuel as I could. Dry wood was a little hard to find in the thick underbrush around us. I took an ax with me and where I could find a fallen tree, used the ax to hack away the bark and outer surface. Any dry sticks in the middle of the underbrush I also dragged with me. I placed what I could find in a pile at the end of the trail.

I moved to my right to expand my search for wood. As I passed the cave mouth above me, immediately to the right of where we'd set up camp, I glanced upward. The curiosity was overwhelming as I searched the wall at the right front of the entrance. Did I see markings there, or was it my imagination and wishful thinking? I glanced over toward the others, then climbed up quickly to the entrance. There was a scratched out half moon shape at eye level in the rock wall. I stared at the carved-out area in the rock and traced my fingers over the shape of it. It was unmistakably hand carved.

One glance outside told me there wasn't much light left, and there would be even less inside. I had no torch or light of any kind to carry inside with me. I turned and hurried inside the cave, letting my eyes adjust to the darkness which only grew as I walked farther back. I saw nothing remarkable as I went deeper into the darkness and rounded a turn, then tripped over something in the gloom. I pulled myself to my feet and saw that I had fallen over a pile of rocks at the edge of the cave floor. I knelt and began pulling rocks away from the pile, stopping to feel inside the cleared area after removing several of the rocks. My fingers encountered something bulky, and I stared through the gathering gloom into the hole I had just created. I could see leather straps and metal edging on a large rectangular object. I explored the size of it, feeling back as far as I could reach. My mind formed the word "strongbox" even as I began replacing the rocks I had removed. I finished recovering my discovery and left the cave. There was plenty of time to explore this in the daylight. I probably wouldn't get any sleep now. No need to tell the others yet. Maybe they could get a good night's sleep. Kate, for one, certainly could use it.

Chapter Thirteen

Seven is a Crowd

For the first time since leaving Cimarron on this trip, Moore was up at daybreak. He made sure the others were also, because this seemed to be turning out as well as he could have possibly hoped. Something was hidden or buried in one of these caves. Whatever it was, they seemed to think they would be able to haul it out on a couple of packhorses. Taking the packhorses from them, along with whatever they were searching for in these caves, should be easy.

They had all searched the cave to the left yesterday afternoon and had come out with nothing. The cave they were in now appeared to be their camp. Reilly had searched the cave to the right briefly as the sun was setting. Moore made sure all three of them had a rifle and ammunition as well as their gun belts, then began shifting everyone toward the right. If they came out of there with anything today, this should be easy.

Sam was up and moving as the dawn broke. The two caves on the left hadn't produced anything, but the third one on the right was still a possibility. Sam moved quickly around the right edge of the gunmen's camp. He needed to be flanking them, with a field of fire away from the caves. Moving quickly through the trees, he'd left his horse tethered back in the woods. This confrontation was going to happen on foot. He heard them moving around now, but he was past them on the right, nearing the caves. He settled into a nest of boulders at the edge of the woods and checked his field of fire. Perfect. He was hidden behind the rocks, but he had a view of the clearing. When he stood, he was covered from the chest down by the boulders, with plenty of room above them to fire. He double-checked the shotgun. Both barrels were loaded. He settled down to wait.

Much to my surprise, I had actually napped a little after Jim spelled me on watch during the night. The small fire we'd used had died down to just a few smoldering embers. Kate had come awake long enough to snuggle over for some warmth. I was picturing life on the double ranch with a full herd. Somewhere during the night, the smile must have faded when I dozed off.

My good mood this morning kept getting better. Kate glanced at me once or twice, then came over to demand an explanation for the huge smile. "I'm a happy guy," I protested. She wouldn't be put off. "I know, but this is something more. Come on. Out with it." She waited with arms folded until I came clean. Well, no use dragging out the suspense any more. "I think I found it last night." "WHAT???" The words came in unison from father and daughter. I explained my brief trip into the cave next door, and box I'd found buried beneath the rocks. Breakfast was forgotten as we scrambled down the face and across to the neighboring cave. Kate, I noticed with approval, stopped long enough to pick up my father's old Henry rifle. Jim and I wore gun belts, but had left our hands free for carrying things. I stopped and returned to the entrance of our cave long enough to pick up my Winchester rifle.

We scrambled up the slope to the cave I'd explored the night before. The morning light was a little stronger now than what I'd had last night, but we still had to move slowly. I set my rifle down just inside the entrance and Kate did likewise. We slowly followed the natural turns before us until we were all standing in front of the pile of rocks I'd seen the night before. I stooped down and began to lift the rocks and set them to the side. Jim and Kate spread out around the rock pile and began to do the same. After a few minutes we could see an old wooden strongbox with metal edges. It was bound by old straps wrapped around it. There was an old hasp with a rusty lock securing it on the side. We lifted it from the floor and carried it around the bend into better light. We all stared at it without speaking.

I reached for my belt and withdrew my knife. Cutting the old straps wrapped around the box took only seconds, but the old rusty lock proved more formidable. We picked up the box and rammed the lock against the cave wall a few times without success. We went back to the rock pile, picked up a couple of rocks apiece and took turns smashing the lock with the rocks. I was about to go back to the packhorses for an ax when the old lock finally yielded. I tore it off and pried it open.

I had a sense of disbelief as I stared into the box. It was filled with gold coins. After twenty years and the death of at least fifteen soldiers, this shipment would finally be delivered. I glanced up at Jim and Kate, each of them lost in their own thoughts. I suspected that Anne Randolph's connection to this shipment might be uppermost in their minds.

Jim and I grabbed a handle apiece and we carried the box out to the cave entrance. We set it down on the cave floor, the gold pieces shining and reflecting the early morning sunlight. I turned to scramble down the face and make the trip over for the packhorses when a movement at the outer edge of my field of vision stopped me. I turned back toward the clearing in front of the caves. Three men stood there; rifles trained on us. I recognized them from Sam's saloon. The one with double tied down guns took a step forward, rifle centered on me. "We'll be taking that chest," he announced. "Ease those gun belts off and put them on the ground."

I took in the situation at a glance—we stood no chance against three rifles already aimed in our direction. I raised my right hand in the air and moved my left hand slowly over to unbuckle the gun belt. Kate remained standing where she was. I couldn't see Jim behind me, but I could only assume he was also moving to unbuckle his gun belt. Suddenly I registered movement to my far left and heard a familiar voice: "I don't think you really need to unbuckle that gun, Chance," Sam said conversationally. "I've got two loaded barrels in this shotgun and I really can't miss whoever I aim at from here. Plus, I've got a side gun myself and I'm behind these boulders here. I'd say you boys need to put those rifles down. You never know which two of you I'll pick out for this shotgun." That was an unusually long speech for Sam but I relished every word of it. I risked a glance over there: he wasn't bluffing. The shotgun was aimed at the one with two tied down guns in the middle, but he wouldn't need to swing it far to get off a second shot.

For several seconds nobody moved. It was beginning to look like a long nerve-wracking standoff. "I'm not a patient man," Sam advised. "You boys need to get moving." At long last, the one on the far right moved slowly to put his rifle on the ground and kick it away. He earned a vicious look from his partners in crime as he slowly unbuckled his gun belt, laid it on the ground and stepped back. "Well now," Sam continued. "Now I have a barrel for each of you boys that haven't let go of your rifles. Ain't that nice. I'm even less patient now than I was before. Move." I swung my gaze back around to the two remaining bandits. The face in the center was a mask of pure rage. The one on the left had me worried a little more. He wore a calculating look on his face. Surely he wasn't crazy enough to risk a direct shotgun blast. Both bent slowly and placed their rifles on the ground.

Sam came around the boulders, shotgun still aimed in the middle. "Back off from those rifles and unbuckle the gun belts," he told them. Both moved to comply. As Sam reached the one in the middle, he bent to pick up the rifle. The gun belt from the man in the middle was already on the ground, but the man on the left was still holding the unbuckled belt. I saw his head jerk upward and he reached for the gun with the right hand just before dropping the belt to the ground. The gun began to clear the holster, but mine was already in my hand. I fired a shot that drove him back several steps. He was still holding the gun as he fell back to his knees. I fired again and he pitched over onto his back, gun dropping away beside him as he fell.

I swung back to the middle. Sam had backed away, shotgun trained again on the one in the middle, who still glared at me. I wasn't sure if this one was crazy or not. The one on the left was greedy and foolish. Had been greedy and foolish, I corrected myself. The one on the right remained rooted where he was, hands in the air. The one in the middle spoke to me: "Looks like you have me covered. Give me a fair fight and I bet things would be a little different." There was hatred in those eyes, but maybe a little fear also. Sam cleared his throat. "Want me to put the shotgun down, Chance?" I shook my head, my eyes never moving from the one in the middle. "No. Somebody has already died needlessly today. I don't have time for you. I'm doing you a favor. Leave the guns. Sam here will walk you back to your horses and make sure you don't have any more weapons. Then you can leave. I indicated the one on the ground with my left hand. Take him with you."

Jim picked up his rifle and went with Sam as they collected their horses where they'd been tethered and walked the two remaining robbers back to the clearing. I sat in the mouth of the cave and watched as they picked up the dead man, threw him over the saddle and tied him down. They walked slowly away, leading the third horse with the body as they disappeared down the trail. I stared at the spot where he'd been just a few minutes before. How many men had I killed now? Kate, reading my mind, sat down next to me and put a comforting arm around me. "There was nothing else you could do. It was you or him." I nodded. "I know. Greed does strange things to people. He had no chance at all against all of us." Kate leaned over to give me a kiss and whispered in my ear. "He had no chance against you, sweetie. Your gun was up and level before he cleared the holster."

I turned to look at her, then looked away. Was that true? I wanted no reputation as a gunman. It attracted other gunmen, many of them crazy young kids trying for a reputation of their own. Was that why the one with two tied down guns had looked at me with a mixture of hatred and fear? I sighed and stood up, turning back to the strongbox we'd left in the middle of the entrance. We would be needing the packhorses. I turned and scrambled down to the base of the cliffs, then walked over to our campsite to bring the packhorses.

The mood lightened as we began to distribute the gold pieces among the saddle bags. The odds had seemed pretty long at times, and now we had what we'd come for. I walked over to Sam as he hung a saddle bag over one of the packhorses. He turned to look at me, and the words I was looking for just didn't come. I looked down and tried again to thank him. Sam adjusted the saddle bag, patted me on the shoulder and walked back toward the strongbox. "Don't get all mushy on me," he said over his shoulder. "Doesn't look like you needed all that much help anyway." I chuckled, shook my head and went to get another empty saddle bag.

The coins turned out to be heavier than we'd expected. Nobody stopped to count them—we had one eye on the trail and the woods around us as we loaded. One surprise a day was more than enough. We spread the coins out on the two packhorses and decided we needed to lighten the load a little, so we took some of the load off each packhorse and spread it among our four horses. Finally satisfied, we led our horses out to the clearing and began to saddle up. When I didn't see Kate, I looked around and saw that she had dragged the strongbox back out to the better light in the mouth of the cave and was exploring the interior of it. Then I saw her stiffen a bit and pull something out of the box.

Kyle Moore pushed his horse down the trail as fast as the branches overlapping the path allowed. His rage built with every step. He looked back once in a while to see if Duke was keeping up. Leading Murchison's horse with the dead body strapped to it was slowing him down. When Duke kept asking to stop and bury the body, he finally agreed, mainly to pick up the pace after the burial. He refused to take a turn digging. He let Duke dig a shallow grave and say a few words, then moved on. He cared about having Duke with him only to the extent they appeared more formidable to any bandits or war parties by having two instead of one. Nobody else would know they had no ammunition.

Just his luck, Moore thought bitterly, that he had thrown his lot in with a fool and a coward. What was Murchison thinking, drawing against all those guns? Probably he had counted on the shotgun being used on Moore and Duke. And he'd thought he could take Reilly. That one hadn't even turned out to be close. Moore had never worried about his ability to take Murchison in a gunfight—he'd seen Murchison in action once before. Even so, Reilly had been extremely fast and accurate. For a moment, he wondered about the personal grudge he now carried toward Reilly. He'd said he didn't have time for Moore. That was an insult that still stung. Moore reflected on his feelings as he'd ridden away. Rage and maybe a hint of fear. Did he fear the result if he'd faced Reilly back there? He dismissed the thought instantly. Reilly was backed by a shotgun and the girl's father, who was still wearing his gun belt at the time. Moore would find a time and place to teach Reilly his lesson. His final lesson. Moore grinned at the thought.

Speaking of the fool and the coward, Moore reined in and let Duke ride up alongside. They were now on the main trail leading back to the Raton Pass road. He estimated they had an hour before reaching the road. As Duke came up alongside, he masked his disgust. This one had caved in and tossed down his rifle when they still had a chance for a standoff. He would deal with Duke in his own time. For now, Moore still had a use for him.

Moore nodded his head in the direction of the Raton Pass road. "We can cross the Canadian River tonight, I'm thinking," he said. "We can be back in Cimarron by tomorrow and get some ammunition and food. We can still take them by surprise and take the gold before they get to town." Duke glanced at him occasionally as he was speaking, then shook his head. "I don't think so," he said finally. Moore looked at him with shock and growing anger. "What? You saw how much gold they had." Duke took in the look on his face, but stubbornly held his ground. "Yeah, but I also saw how much of it Murchison won't be spending. I won't shoot a man from ambush and I'm not a big enough fool to take on Reilly. I expect I'll be riding the other direction when we get to the road."

Moore reacted in equal parts to the statement about shooting from ambush and to the comment that showed fear at the idea of bracing Reilly. His hand moved almost imperceptibly toward the knife in his belt. Duke saw the movement and backed his horse fractionally. Element of surprise gone; Moore relaxed a little in the saddle. He wasn't all that good with a knife and he didn't fancy getting rid of the body. He knew the anger still showed in his face, but one look at the stubborn set on Duke's face told him this was a final decision. Moore backed his horse and swung it around. "I'm going on," he hissed over his shoulder. "You wait here till I'm out of sight. If I see you around Cimarron, I'll kill you. I can't abide a coward."

Duke didn't doubt for a minute the threat from Moore. He sat his horse in the path until Moore was out of sight, then waited another half hour. He took his time reaching the road to Raton Pass. He looked to his right as he reached the road, then swung his horse to the left. Maybe he could join up with another traveler or two before he got to Trinidad to buy some ammunition and food. Then maybe he would ride on out toward Dodge City and beyond to look for some work. An honest living was suddenly sounding better. He kicked his horse into a canter and headed north.

Chapter Fourteen

Anne Randolph

Her horse saddled and ready, Kate scrambled back up the slope and into the mouth of the cave to retrieve the Henry rifle. It wasn't as light as the rifle she'd had before, but she'd grown comfortable with it. It reminded her a little of Chance's dad. She had only vague memories of him, but they were good memories. As she picked up the rifle and turned to leave, her eyes fell on the discarded strongbox laying at the edge of the entrance. She stooped over it and idly ran her fingers along the interior and edges of the box. It was made of solid oak with a rough burlap lining on the inside. Something struck her as usual about the lining, so she dragged the box out to the front edge of the cave entrance for a better look.

She knelt down next to the box, looking for the rip in the lining she thought she'd felt inside. She turned the box in the light, exploring the edges of the lining with her fingers. There! Her fingers encountered a small rip at the top edge of the lining. She ran her fingers inside and explored the wooden surface inside, but feel anything other than the wooden wall of the box. She prepared to stand up and leave, pulling the lining away from the edge as she did so, looking into the bottom of the box. She stopped and knelt by the box again. There was a scrap of paper on the bottom, underneath the lining.

She reached in, ripping the lining a little farther in order to reach the note. She pulled it out, noticing that it was yellow with age. She unfolded the paper, spreading it out in the sunshine and seeing there was a note handwritten in faded, smudged pencil. She read it twice before the meaning of it dawned on her. She read it the third time; eyes wide with shock. It had been written by her mother:

the apaches have us surrounded. George says they will kill him

but might take me prisoner. help me.   Anne Randolph

I reached Kate in the mouth of the cave. I found her holding a scrap of paper, shock etched in her features. She didn't answer my obvious question about the paper, she simply passed it to me wordlessly. As I took it, I glanced into the strongbox. The lining was ripped; it seemed clear she had found the note inside. I read it twice before the full import dawned on me. I passed it back to Kate, as wordless as she was. I motioned for Jim and Sam to come up and join us. Both shrugged, tethered the horses and climbed up to the cave. We passed the note around.

We were all sitting in a semicircle at the cave entrance, absorbing the meaning of the note. It now seemed likely Kate had seen her mother just the day before yesterday. Jim was the first to speak. "I can't speak for you, Chance and Sam, but I can speak for myself and I'm pretty sure for Kate." He glanced at her sideways before continuing. "We have to go find her if we can. If there's just the two of us, we can't try a rescue, but if we know where she is, we could tell the army... "His voice trailed away as Kate nodded her agreement.

"I'm in," I interrupted. You and Kate are my family too, now, so I'm in." Sam levered himself to a standing position, using his shotgun as a crutch. He winced a little at the pain in his side. "I don't know about family, but I'm not crazy enough to get left out of something like this," he said, with a small sardonic grin on his face. "If that was her, she's been a prisoner long enough. Let's go get her." Kate stood and enveloped us both with a hug, thanking us in low tones. Jim stood a bit to the side, eyes a little misty, seemingly at a loss for words.

Talk then turned to how we would locate her. "Kate," I asked. "Where were you when you crossed paths with the other group?" "Do you think the four warriors who took you were part of the same band?" She knitted her brows in thought for a moment. "I think they were very familiar with each other, so yes, I think they may have been a part of the same band. We met up in the clearing where you came to get me yesterday. The larger group with the woman captive moved away to the north."

"So, we have a starting point," I observed. "And maybe the four who took Kate were a hunting party for the whole band. They just didn't hesitate to take a captive when they saw the chance. We can retrace our steps to where we were yesterday and see if we can track them." I looked around and saw slow nods of agreement.

Jim offered a sobering thought: "The four warriors who took Kate might not be the only hunting party for that band. I'd bet there's a good chance there's another group, looking for some food to bring with them when they set up a camp for the summer." I filed the thought away. Sheer numbers would probably require us to do something different to rescue Anne, assuming we could even find her.

Sam spoke up for the first time. "They had a couple places north of here where they used to set up camps when the weather turned warmer. That would be about now. I used to trap in that area, but only during the winter. Warmer weather meant too many of them around and I valued my hair too much. If we lose them when we're trying to track, my memory might be good enough to get us to their campground. I want to throw in my two cents with what Jim said, though—there's likely to be more warriors when we find them. They are not likely to be the peaceful, non-threatening bunch that moved out a couple days ago."

Sam and Jim had kept the guns belonging to the dead man, and all the ammunition the three of them had in their camp. They had left the two remaining men enough food to last them for the trip to Trinidad, which was where they claimed to be going. The extra food kept by Sam and Jim would be of great help to us. We hadn't brought enough for an extended trip, which this could now turn out to be.

We generally agreed to retrace our steps to where we had rescued Kate and talk about it again. If there was a clear enough trail to the north, that was our starting point. In any case, we would probably have a better idea once we'd looked the ground over a little better. We mounted up and followed the same trail we'd been on before, looking for Anne Randolph. We could only hope that it was Anne whom Kate had seen two days ago.

Anne Randolph dipped the buckskin shirt in the river and resumed scrubbing it. She had been a part of this Jicarilla Apache tribe for so long that she rarely thought of her given name in that prior life. Among the Apaches in this band she was simply called Snow, because of her light skin. She wore a perpetual tan now because of the life lived outdoors these many years, but still, her skin was much lighter than what these people were used to seeing. She had thought back to her prior life this morning because she had heard the other women discussing another white woman a few hours ago.

Something unusual had happened yesterday. For the most part, she was accepted as another member of the tribe. Indeed, thoughts of escape had disappeared some years ago after a fruitless attempt or two. She knew then that another failed attempt would cost her life. So now she simply fit in, did her job, and was accepted. Once in a while, though, she knew she was being shielded from events or conversations, and these last couple days had been like that. Yesterday she had been hustled away from the camp, and the other squaws and an old man or two had walked very close to her, as if to keep her from being seen. This morning, before going to the river to wash the shirts, she had overheard the native words for "captive" and other words that referred to a white female. They had stopped talking when they realized she might be able to hear.

She resumed scrubbing the shirt on a rock, glancing around to see if anyone was watching her. No one was. In fact, everything seemed to be returning to normal. If that was another captive woman, she must have been with the small hunting party they'd left behind two days ago. She finished with the shirt, wrung it out, and tossed it on a pile with a couple others. She grabbed the next shirt and dipped it in the river. Washing and cooking were her duties now. When she'd first been taken captive, she had been given to a warrior as his squaw. They had been together for about five years. After those attempts at escape, and after accepting her punishment for those efforts, she had resigned herself to the life. She had been treated well enough by the warrior, at least according to their customs, but she had been unable to bear him a child. He had been killed in a skirmish with a cavalry troop.

After the death of her first Apache husband, she had been given to a much older man, whose warrior days were behind him. She had always assumed this was because she'd been unable to bear a child to the younger warrior. Given her resignation to her new life, however, she didn't mind so much being the squaw of warrior who was twenty-five years older. He mainly seemed to want her to do the work he didn't want to do, which was almost all the work needed. She set up the camp, broke it down when they moved, cleaned and prepared any food he could catch or shoot. She made his clothes, mended them, and washed them. Beyond that, he didn't seem to have any expectations of her and they mostly left each other alone. He'd been unable to survive a brutally cold winter two season ago, probably because of old age. Now she wouldn't be given as a squaw to anyone else because of her age, but she could still do her share of work around the camp. It was her life as she'd come to know it, and she accepted it for the most part.

She almost never thought back to the day when she'd been taken captive, but the events of these last two days had exerted an unusual effect on her. Leaving Jim and their daughter had been the biggest mistake of her life, but like all mistakes, she couldn't undo it. She could barely bring herself to think of Kate by her name. She could only think in terms of her daughter with Jim. She hoped they'd been able to have a good life without her. She had been so young, so unprepared for life in the West, and so foolish to listen to the words of that young runaway soldier.

George Gibson had come to their door, and she'd felt sorry for him. He simply worked around the ranch with Jim for a week or so, but then began finding more and more opportunities to talk to her when Jim wasn't around. He talked about an enormous amount of money he was going to recover soon, and how he would take that money to San Francisco to live the good life. She'd never been to San Francisco, but his description of the city sounded like everything she'd ever wanted, so far away from this lonely life in Cimarron. And then he'd begun to talk about how she could come with him and live that same life. In the end, it was too much for the young Anne Randolph to resist.

Everything had gone bad, almost from the beginning. She had left a note for Jim and slipped away from the ranch when Jim and Kate were gone from the house. She had taken the trail around the town of Cimarron to avoid being seen, and had met up with George Gibson on the other side of town. His memory of how to retrace his steps to the gold had been poor. She had guided him to the Canadian River crossing, because he was sure it was north of there. They had eventually found their way to the pine tree struck by lightning, although it had been time consuming and they hadn't brought enough food. The fact that Gibson had shot a deer for food had probably been the start of their downfall. It had most likely alerted the Apaches to their presence in the area.

Finding the game trail back to the cliffs had taken a full day. After shooting the deer that second morning, Gibson had been looking over his shoulder constantly. She began to feed off his nervousness and any noise in the woods had sent her heart into her mouth. It seemed an eternity had passed before he felt confident he'd found the trail. Afraid of pursuit, they had abandoned any attempt at silence and rushed down the game trail for the comparative safety of a cave. By the time they actually gained the entrance of the cave and led their horses in, a war party had encircled them. A few arrows found their way into the cave, and one of them had killed George's horse. They had used the horse to shield them, and had spent a long night on guard, firing an occasional shot over the corpse and into the trees. They both knew it was just a matter of time.

As the morning light began to filter in, he'd told her they would come with the first light and the two of them wouldn't be able to hold the Apaches off for very long. He'd told her they would kill him, but might spare her life and take her as a captive. That hadn't sounded a lot better than death. She'd come up with the idea of leaving a note in the strongbox and burying the box back in the pile of rocks, in the hope that a search party would find it. As long as the Apaches didn't carry it away, it at least seemed like a possibility. He supplied her with a pencil and paper. She had written the note, then ripped the lining of the box to hide the note, just in case the Apaches found the box. It seemed like a small, useless gesture, but it was all she had. She put the box back where it had been and covered it back over with rocks.

Returning to the mouth of the cave, she had arrived just in time to see George Gibson put his gun to his temple and use the last bullet on himself. It was an image she had never been able to get out of her mind. As he had guessed, they had taken her prisoner, tied her up and carried her off with them.

Anne came out of her trance-like memories to realize that she had finished the shirts, and one of the other squaws was approaching, looking at her and gesturing for her to return to the camp. She tossed the last shirt on the pile, picked up the load and followed the other squaw back to the clearing. Teepees were being taken down. It looked like they were moving again, probably going to the higher mountain pasture where they sometimes made camp for the summer.

The clearing where we'd rescued Kate looked completely different in the daylight, deserted and empty. They had taken their dead with them, and there was nothing left from the battle we'd had there only two days before. We scouted the perimeter of the area, finding only a few faint tracks leading off to the north and west. It wasn't much to go on, but it was all we had. We estimated, based on the timeline provided by Kate, that the larger group had left this area three days before. We decided to camp at the outlook that Jim had used to fire down into the clearing. The higher ground felt more secure. Uppermost in our minds was the possibility there was another war party/hunting party attached to this same band of the Apaches.

Kate and I snuggled up by the remnants of our cooking fire after Sam and Jim had retired for the evening, talking about whether or not it was possible that the woman she'd seen was her mother. We talked for the first time about the difficulty of getting her away from this larger band. Would she even cooperate with being rescued? We couldn't really come sweeping in there the way I had come to get Kate. She wouldn't even know who I was. Why would she go with me? There was no way she would recognize Kate. Jim was the only one she might recognize on sight, but twenty years had passed since she had seen him.

Try as we might, we couldn't come up even with the outline of a plan we felt would work. Too much depended on the circumstances we would be in if and when we found Kate's mother. We could only take one step at a time, we concluded. First, we had to try to find her. Then we had to hope that circumstances would suggest a plan for us. As the night air grew colder, we pulled a couple blankets around us and watched the last of the embers die out. Tomorrow was step one—we had to pool our skills to track the group that had left here two days ago. Step two would be something to worry about after step one. Somewhere along the way, we leaned back onto the ground and fell asleep.

Chapter Fifteen

Tracking Ghosts

Luckily there hadn't been any rain in recent days, making it easier to follow the tracks we found leading north and west from the clearing. It didn't seem like they had made any particular effort to cover the tracks, but wild game crossing or following the trail had obscured things a bit by this point. We followed their tracks successfully for the first morning, but then our luck ran out. The trail seemed to disappear into the woods, and following any kind of trail through the underbrush didn't seem possible. We had no doubt they had passed through to this point, and had probably gone on through these woods, but they left us no trace of their passing.

We dismounted at the end of the trail and had a small meal while we considered the possibilities. No one was in a mood to go home, but nobody wanted to press forward blindly through unfamiliar territory. Finally, Sam offered us a ray of hope. "They'll need water," he pointed out. "Wherever they're going to end up, which is probably in a camp up there—," he nodded toward the mountains, "their most immediate need is going to be water. We can push forward in the direction we've been going; we keep our eyes open for water. Ears, too. Sometimes a mountain stream can run down into a pool of water. Where we find water, maybe we can strike tracks again."

We spread out in a thin line and began to push through the trees and underbrush. In the army, we'd have called it a skirmish line, and that didn't seem so inaccurate if we should run into surprises out here. I kept one hand on the Colt 45 in my holster and I was never far from the Winchester I had in a scabbard on Archie. We were definitely not going to be viewed as friendly if we were found out here. Finally, by mid-afternoon we struck a small trickle of water running downhill from the mountains in front of us. We changed direction slightly to follow the stream of water, which was growing in size as we moved higher up into the foothills in front of us. By evening, we found a small pool of water, no doubt dammed up by the beavers in the area. Around the pool of water, there were numerous tracks of unshod ponies.

We stopped to water our horses and refill canteens, and with the sun beginning to set, we decided to pull well back from the water pool and make a camp without fire for the night. We found a small clearing several hundred yards back from the pool that we decided would be our camp. We debated our next move, speaking almost in whispers and listening to the night sounds around us. Sam and Jim were both of the opinion we may be fairly close to one of the summer camping grounds this band might use. If we were lucky, we might be close enough that one or more of them would come back here for water and lead us to them. It was worth the wait of a half-day or so to see if that would happen. We turned in early after dragging a log into the clearing and turning it for shelter against the north wind coming off the mountains. Just to be safe, we also dragged some dead branches and pine needles over our blankets for camouflage before drifting off to sleep.

I awoke to a dim gray light filtering through the juniper trees above me. It took me a moment to orient myself. Kate lay next to me, breathing evenly and quietly. I raised my head just slightly to see that both Sam and Jim were also still asleep. I took a moment to listen before moving any farther. Listening carefully in the silence, I thought maybe I could hear the slight sound of water moving or dripping, but couldn't be sure. I slowly raised my head over the log and saw what looked like a hunting party of five Jicarilla Apaches watering their ponies at the pool. I froze where I lay, hoping that nobody else would choose this moment to wake up. All five were on one knee at the edge of the water, drinking from cupped hands.

They finished watering their horses, then dipped some animal skins in the pool to fill those with water. I counted three stripped deer carcasses tied to their ponies. I looked carefully at the weapons they were carrying: I saw one rifle, probably a very old Spencer. Beyond that, I saw only bows and arrows, as well as the usual tomahawks and knives. They conversed in low tones for a few minutes, taking stock of their surroundings, then mounted up and splashed through the pool, moving off to the northwest. I exhaled for what felt like the first time in ten minutes, then lay without moving while I waited for the others to wake up. When they finally began to stir, I moved around to each of them and whispered a warning to stay as quiet as possible.

We really had only a few ways to proceed now. We could retreat, rather than chance running into the hunting party, then let the army know that we believed there was a white captive up here. We had come too far for that to be appealing to anybody. Another choice, trying to closely follow a band of Apache warriors was far too risky. We had some outdoor and tracking skills, but we didn't kid ourselves we had enough for that. The Apaches were master trackers and woodsmen. The only other choice was to wait a half day or so for them to move on, then see if we could follow this more recent trail left for us, hopefully for only a short time, with them leading us to where Anne Randolph was being held. I had watched them leave heading northwest, so we had a starting point. For lack of any better choices, we picked option three and prepared to leave. We broke camp around midday, splashed through the pool and began a slow climb into the mountains.

Kyle Moore sat his horse in the trees just off the trail, waiting to see if Duke tried to follow him to Cimarron. He didn't trust having Duke around him, for starters, and he couldn't abide anyone telling a story around town that he had backed down for Reilly. His anger continued to burn at that thought. He would take care of Reilly in due time, but Duke was his first concern. Finally satisfied that he was the only one on the road back to Cimarron, he pulled his horse out from the trees and headed for the Canadian River crossing. He had time to get to Cimarron by tomorrow, and that was the deadline he was giving himself for what he had in mind.

Late afternoon the next day found him getting close to Cimarron. He pulled off the trail to decide what he wanted to do next. They hadn't taken his money back there—he couldn't believe that. He had enough in his pockets, plus something he'd buried just outside of town from his last robbery, to last him a couple weeks in town. Plus, he figured he had enough to restock his ammunition. Leaving him the money was going to cost them. He decided he would go back to the hotel in Cimarron. The only person from the town that seemed to suspect him of anything was the old man at the saloon, and he obviously wasn't there right now. They didn't even have a sheriff. This should be easy. As he took the trail on into town, he kept a sharp eye out for a good place to set up an ambush. Nothing caught his eye on the first pass, but he had some time yet to set it up.

Riding on into town, he checked in at the hotel, had a bath and a meal, then went over to the general store to buy his ammunition. He tied up his horse and pushed through the doors, remembering at the last minute that the owner's name was Purvis. Sometimes a little chit-chat kept people at ease, and he might need that. After a few words about the weather and things around town, Moore got around to ordering several boxes of ammunition for both his Winchester rifle and Navy Colt revolver. Purvis stacked the boxes on the counter and looked at him for the first time with a questioning glance. Moore managed a disarming grin. "Buying for my partner, too," he said. "He'll be along in a couple days." The store owner seemed only partly assured. "Just one partner? I thought there were three of you before." Moore cursed under his breath, but managed another reassuring smile. "There were, that's right. One decided to try his luck up Dodge City way." That was a true enough statement. Purvis nodded and completed the sale without further comment. Feeling the store owner's eyes still on his back, he loaded the ammunition on his horse, moved him to the hitching rack in front of the hotel and unloaded most of it. He would find an ambush spot later and transport some of it out there when nobody was watching.

He hesitated outside the store, glancing over toward the saloon. The old saloon keeper was still gone. He crossed the street and went inside, not seeing anybody he knew. He sat by himself at the window, watching passersby on the street and tossing down a couple whiskeys served by the fresh-faced kid behind the bar. He asked about the old saloon keeper, but got only a shrug in reply. He decided not to push it any farther. They'd be back with the gold soon enough.

Mounting up and moving out north of town, he began again to look for an ambush spot. He rode a couple miles before he even began to look. He didn't need the people in the town riding out to investigate gunshots. He would have to be well down the road toward Trinidad before anybody knew anything back in Cimarron. After a couple miles, be began to look for a place, concentrating on the western side of the road. If he was lucky enough to catch them with the setting sun in their eyes, so much the better. Also, better to catch them coming around a bend in the trail. He knew from experience they would have a shorter reaction time if the turn in the road blocked their view.

After another mile had gone by, he saw a likely possibility. He reined in and surveyed it from where he sat, then rode down to a turn in the trail and looked back from that vantage point. He grunted briefly in satisfaction. A thick stand of trees pretty much blocked the view, which was perfect. He rode back, dismounted, and began to investigate on foot. A fallen tree gave shelter and a resting place for his rifle. He knelt behind the tree and swung his rifle back and forth across the log to make sure he could cover the road completely. He could, with no gaps in his field of fire. Satisfied, he sat back, rifle still in hand, and pictured how he could do this.

The old saloon keeper would likely still have that shotgun. He would have to take out the old man first. Then Reilly. As much as he would like to cut Reilly down man-to-man, he wanted to get away with that gold even more. So, Reilly would have to go down with the second shot. With some luck, he could take out the girl's father before the last two could find shelter in the woods or behind a horse. That would just leave the girl. She might just give up the gold at that point without a shot fired. It didn't matter if she did. He would have to kill her too. Nobody could be left behind to tell about this.

Satisfied, he dug a hole behind the log and buried some of the ammunition he'd brought out. Maybe he would just leave the rifle here tomorrow as well. He didn't need to rouse suspicion by riding in and out of town packing his rifle each day. He kicked some dirt over the tracks he'd left coming in, and made sure he could recognize this spot from the road when he returned. Tomorrow morning was soon enough to set himself up in his hideaway and start watching for their return.

The morning chill became more noticeable the higher we rode, and I turned up my collar against the northern breezes sweeping down on us. We were able to rely on my memory for the first part of the ride this morning. I had clearly seen the Jicarilla Apaches splash through the pool and scatter out a bit as they rode up the hillside, crested the rise and disappeared on the other side. We wasted no time moving up to the rise where I'd last seen them, but from there we dismounted, spread out, and proceeded slowly on foot. We felt confident we'd not been seen so far, but if they spotted us and doubled back behind us, we were in a lot of trouble.

Jim angled his way over to me as we continued on foot downhill. From time to time a broken twig or single hoofprint assured us we were still on the right track. Jim fell alongside me as we walked, voicing his doubts about whether Anne would even come with us voluntarily after these many years. I nodded, glancing over at him. "Kate and I had a discussion like this last night. I can't just go sneaking in there like last time. She doesn't know me. We don't figure she'd have any way to recognize Kate after all this time. You're the only one she's likely to recognize on sight, and even that might take a while. On top of that, we need to get a good enough look first to feel sure it's Anne." Jim stared ahead quietly, and I could almost feel the hope draining out of him. I decided to change course with the conversation. "First, we'll find her," I told him. "We can watch the camp when we find it and we'll take as much time as we need to be sure it's her. Then we'll figure out how to get her out." Jim cast a grateful glance in my direction and moved over to cover more ground again in the search for tracks. "Thanks, son," I heard him say in an undertone as he walked away.

By afternoon we knew they had put some distance between us. There was still an occasional track to keep us going. In addition, there were mostly just sheer rock faces and cliffs to our north, meaning they were unlikely to be passing in that direction. Besides, the land in front of us in the northwesterly direction we had chosen seemed to alternate rises and valleys in a gentler climb. That seemed more promising if they were looking to settle down for the summer up here somewhere. By late afternoon we had run across a mountain stream rushing through the rocks and cutting across a valley below. We watered our horses, then began working up and down the muddy banks of the river, looking for tracks. We found them a little to the north of where we were, so they had veered a little off the course we'd be taking, but we felt confident now we were back on the trail.

The new angle we'd taken had us climbing at a steeper angle, and we sensed we might be approaching a crest. Our horizon seemed to be getting closer and closer, indicating a ridge might be cutting off our view. The late afternoon sun was in our eyes as we climbed, and we became more uneasy with the thought of sky lining ourselves in the setting sun if we kept going. I motioned for the others to pull together for a quick conference and made a proposal. "If you want to stay here and hold on to Archie, I'll go forward by myself until I get a better look at what's in front of us," I said. "If that's a ridge up there in front of us, I'd rather cross over it in early morning light. I just want a peek at what we're dealing with up there. If anybody has a better idea, let me know." I looked around. Sam gave the reins for his horse to Kate and said "I'm coming with you." Jim and Kate nodded agreement. I pulled my Winchester from the saddle and Sam opted for the shotgun. We began working our way up the hill.

We toiled up the slope in silence for a half hour or so when Sam stopped and held me back with a hand on my arm. "Do you smell smoke?" he asked. I stopped and tested the wind, breathing in deeply. I nodded. We dropped to our knees and crawled forward until we had topped the rise and looked down into a valley below. There were a dozen teepees or so and a few small campfires. I counted briefly and estimated a total of twenty or so people. We had found an Apache encampment. It remained to be seen whether we'd found the one we were looking for. We observed for a few minutes, then backed away down the hill, eventually getting back on our feet and walking back to rejoin the others.

Chapter Sixteen

Man on a Sorrel Horse

We all lay flat on our stomachs, hugging to the ground with a few rocks and boulders to give a little extra cover at the top of the ridge. We had made sure no one was wearing anything reflective. With the morning sun at our backs, we made use of Sam's binoculars, covering them with a rag to prevent glare off any metallic surface on them. I looked down into the encampment, counting. I made it to be eighteen people. There were the five warriors we had followed to get here, five older males past any age to be considered a warrior, four squaws and four children, all probably younger than about eight years of age. It was beginning to sink in what a difficult task this would be. We were outnumbered by the warriors alone, and I wasn't discounting how much damage the older men and squaws could do to us also.

I lowered my head for a moment and stared at the ground in front of me, trying to visualize a way in and out of that camp. I raised my head again slightly, memorizing the layout. The camp was set in a clearing in front of us. A mountain stream cut across the far side of the camp. Trees ringed the clearing on all three sides in front of us. On the far side, the ground rose fairly steeply toward the mountains behind it. On the right were cliffs and rocky faces, making it almost impossible to travel in that direction. On the left was a bit of a slope climbing up to another outcropping overlooking the camp. It didn't provide concealment and protection quite as good as the spot we were on, but we could use that for observation also if needed.

I looked back down into the camp and saw that two of the women had carried things down to the stream. I couldn't tell from here if they were dipping clothes in the river or washing some kind of food—maybe roots or berries. Jim lay next to me with the binoculars, and he watched the women intently. For the most part, they had their backs to us, but finally finished what they were doing and turned their faces in our directions as they came back and disappeared into a teepee. Their heads were tilted down the whole time they faced us. I looked over at Jim and waited for the verdict. He set the binoculars down in frustration. "Maybe," he whispered finally. "One of them could have been her, but I just couldn't get a good enough look." He cast his gaze on the outcropping to the left. "Do you think we could get a look from up there?"

We wormed our way back down the slope and into the tree line behind us. Once we were concealed by the trees and underbrush, we began to move off to our left. We had maybe two hours before the overhead western sun might start to reflect off those binoculars, and we hated to lose the rest of the day. There was less cover at the top of this embankment, so only Jim and I crawled up to the top. Sam and Kate kept their rifles handy and stood guard on either side of us, one to each side.

Time passed slowly with almost nothing happening down there as the sun climbed higher overhead. I look up anxiously and back down to the binoculars. We had just a little time left before we would have to call it quits for today. Jim lay motionless, fixated on the camp below us. Finally, at the teepee closest to us, one of the older men started a fire and two of the squaws came out, bringing meat toward the campfire. Even from up here and without the binoculars, I could tell that one of the two had a lighter complexion and hair a couple shades lighter than the other one. I glance over at Jim and saw him adjusting the binoculars slightly as he focused in on her. I heard a sharp intake of breath and saw him stiffen. His head came up a little and he continued to stare at her without the binoculars. Then he abruptly began to back down the slope, motioning for me to follow.

He continued on down, past Kate and Sam, and we all trailed him back down to where we'd made camp in the trees. He paced back and forth, his mouth forming words that didn't come until he stopped and stared at Kate. By then, we all knew what he would say. "It's her!! It's her!! I'm sure of it." He turned and continued to pace until Kate turned him slightly and enveloped him in a hug. "We'll get her Dad," Kate said. She looked at me over his shoulder and I knew I would do whatever it took. "We'll get her," Kate repeated.

Now we were down to the hard part. It had been one thing to rescue Kate from the small band a few days ago. They had all been young warriors, but there were only four of them and Kate had been a willing, helping participant. Now there were five warriors along with nine or so others in with the older men and squaws.

They could all do us quite a bit of damage if we took them for granted. And the biggest wildcard of all was Anne herself. How would she react to a rescue attempt? We had no chance at all unless she wanted this and would help us.

We reviewed everything we had to work with. Their campsite afforded us protection in the woods to the west. To the south and east we had an overlook from which we could lay down a field of fire. We quickly eliminated using the overlook to the east. Even though it was a bit higher and afforded better protection, we would probably need someone in the woods to the west and we couldn't take the chance of firing on ourselves. The north was not a consideration. The cliffs in that direction were pretty much impassable.

We knew that Anne was kept busy mainly with cooking, washing and mending clothes, and occasionally with watching the small children. This kept her pretty much in the camp. The farthest she had ventured away was to the stream running through the western edge of the camp. We also realized that the only one of us she might recognize would be Jim. We weren't certain that she would voluntarily come with him in a rescue effort, but we thought she would. The rest of us, including Kate, she wouldn't even know.

From there, we were able to boil things down to a plan that we hoped would work. That plan involved getting Jim close enough to her that she could recognize him and slip away with him unnoticed. Given that she was sometimes down at the stream by herself, or at least with nobody in the immediate area, we had hopes that Jim could work his way down through the trees to the west and get her attention. It was miles away from foolproof, but it was considerably better than anything else we had. Everything else came down to riding in with guns blazing and trying to sweep her up on one of the horses on our way through the camp.

It was decided that Jim would come down on foot through the trees at the southwestern edge of the camp, close to the southern overlook where Sam and Kate would be stationed with rifles. Jim would try to slip away with her, back into the trees. There he would mount up and ride around to join Sam and Kate south of the camp. I would be on horseback in the trees further along on the western edge, working as a backstop in case anything went wrong, basically. If Jim came under fire or was unable to get back to his horse, I would be close enough to give him some help. We debated whether I should try to talk to Anne if she came close enough, but decided against it. She wouldn't know me or have any reason to trust me.

We decided to put the plan into action starting the next morning. We would get to our positions in the early dawn hours and wait for a chance to make things happen. We didn't know how many days it might take to have a situation we could take advantage of, so we planned to start as soon as possible.

Anne emerged from the teepee that morning knowing that today was a rarity for her—a day she looked forward to. The hunting party had returned with three large deer carcasses, and almost as important, three deerskins. She had become quite skilled over the years at making buckskin clothes for the tribe, and today she would make some clothes for the kids. She valued solitude, and she would be left unbothered if she went down to the river, sat on a rock and made the clothes.

She was joined this morning by the one friend she had in the camp, another woman named Wading Bird, who was coming down to the stream to do some washing. They didn't talk all that much, but Anne had come to enjoy the company of the younger woman. They reached the stream and Anne waded across to seat herself on a rock on the other side. She reached for one of the hides and began working. Wading Bird walked along the other bank for ten or fifteen yards and began washing.

The sun became warm on her back as it rose higher over the trees, and it seemed the morning was passing quickly. She thought she heard rustling in the trees behind her from time to time, but decided each time after glancing back that it was only the wind rustling the tree limbs. She glanced over at Wading Bird, who hadn't looked up. As Anne bent to her task, her head came up very suddenly when a small rock landed only a few feet from where she sat. She started to spin around and look into the woods when she was stopped short by the sound of something she hadn't heard in twenty-five years: Her own name! She uttered an involuntary gasp of surprise.

We were up before dawn and took up our positions as we had discussed the day before. Sam and Kate were on the southern overlook spots, rifles at the ready. The ground rose up unevenly from the pasture where the camp lay, with some loose gravel and rock, but it seemed possible to ride up to the overlook from the camp if that were necessary. The height and rocks at the top would offer protection if the Apaches were to attack in that direction. Jim tethered his horse back in the woods but near the overlook where Kate and Sam were stationed. I drifted farther north in the woods, remaining on horseback and observing the camp.

Early on, we got an unexpected break. Two of the warriors caught up horses and rode away to the west. I assumed they had gone to look for more game. Each was armed only with bow and arrow, so that meant the rifle was still in the camp. Still, it helped to even the odds considerably. My spirits rose. I was even more encouraged when I saw Anne, accompanied by one of the other women, walk down to the stream. Anne crossed the stream and sat down on a rock, apparently sewing some clothes. The other woman walked downstream a bit and began washing. Surely, I thought, today is our day.

I watched from my vantage point as Jim worked his way closer and closer through the trees. He reached a spot behind a large pine tree and seemed to settle down back there, leaning around the tree from time to time. I assumed he was trying to get Anne's attention. She glanced behind her once in a while, but always turned back around and resumed working. I shifted my glance to the squaw who had accompanied her, but she remained head down at her work.

I held my breath as I saw Jim pick up a small rock and toss it in Anne's direction. It bounced near her and she swung around. I gathered up Archie's reins and leaned forward in the saddle, watching as Anne stopped, her face registering surprise, maybe even shock. Time seemed to stop for just a moment, and then pandemonium broke loose.

The other woman at the river jumped to her feet and spotted Jim in the woods. She pointed and cut loose an ear-shattering scream as a warning to the others. Anne jumped to her feet and started running toward me, away from Jim. Jim took a few steps in her direction, but a warrior carrying their one rifle appeared from inside a teepee. He took quick aim at Jim and cut loose a shot that missed. An answering boom came from the outlook. The warrior dropped limply to the ground, the rifle bouncing in front of him. The other two warriors appeared from nowhere and began running toward Jim. They gained the shelter of the trees before Sam or Kate could fire on them. Jim reversed course and headed for his horse, but I could see he was going to need help.

Meanwhile, Anne continued to run in my direction. The others all seemed to be headed away from the gunfire coming from the outlook. I surveyed the situation in front of me. Jim needed my help to get those warriors away from him. And, it seemed to me, I could at the same time make one make-or-break effort to get Anne out of there. I kicked Archie hard in the ribs. He leaped forward in surprise and we burst out from the trees. I fired my pistol in the air to draw attention away from the others.

Anne was moving before she could register what had happened. Hearing her name had been a shock, then Wading Bird screamed and rifle fire sounded. She instinctively ran away from the gunfire, splashing through the stream and climbing out for better footing. She saw most of the band moving away from the sound of the shots and toward the cliffs at the far end.

Her mind still struggled to process what had happened. She had heard her own name. Where had that come from? She didn't recognize a voice, but it had been said in a loud whisper, so it probably wouldn't sound familiar, anyway. Wading Bird's scream had gotten her moving, but what was she doing? What if someone had come to take her out of here? She thought back to her attempts at escape many years ago, and the punishment she had endured because of them. She wanted no more of that. She settled down to run for the far cliffs when she heard it again, but this time it came in a scream: "ANNE RANDOLPH!"

She looked up to see a young, dark-haired man on a sorrel horse burst out of the woods, riding directly toward her. His arm was extended to her. She turned away and started to run, then stopped dead in her tracks, looking back at the sight of the man on the sorrel horse. He seemed to have come from nowhere. She reacted impulsively for reasons she was never quite able to understand or explain later on. She swung back, lifted her hand and locked it around the arm of the young man charging down to meet her.

Chapter Seventeen

Escape

Things were unfolding in front of me at increasing speed as I rode out of the woods. To my left, I saw most of the Apache camp running on foot toward the cliffs on the northern side. The children, women other than Anne, and at least most of the older men all seemed to be moving in that direction. One warrior was down, shot from the overlook. The other two still in camp had reached the cover of the trees and were pursuing Jim. When I fired my pistol, they stopped and began moving in my direction. Anne Randolph had splashed through the creek and seemed to be moving toward the northern cliffs. I screamed her name and she stopped to look at me. She hesitated, then turned to run away from me.

I urged Archie forward, frustration sweeping over me. I glanced to see the two warriors taking cover under the face of the southern outlook, angling to cut off my escape in that direction. I screamed Anne's name again and extended my arm to her as I closed the gap between us. She turned toward me, and I could read the indecision on her face. As I raced up to meet her, she threw her arm up and grabbed mine firmly just below the elbow. I turned and swung my arm back as hard as I could while I kept Archie racing forward. Anne did the rest, swinging and kicking hard to clear the ground. She grabbed the back of the saddle and swung herself aboard, then encircled my waist with her arms and hung on.

I could see that Jim had reached his horse and was moving to meet us at the southern overlook. I swept my gaze back to the ground between here and there, worried about those two warriors who had moved to cut me off. I changed course slightly to my right to head for a path I could see leading up the embankment. As we passed a boulder at the base, one of the warriors came up from the ground, tomahawk in the air. I pulled Archie's reins hard to the left, causing him to swerve and strike the warrior full in the chest with his shoulder. I put a shot into him as he spun away to the ground.

Now I could see the other warrior climbing on top of a boulder to my right, notching an arrow. Anne's voice screamed *"Duck!"* in my ear and I laid my head down as far as I could over Archie's neck. There was a whistling noise and I felt the burn of the arrow across the back of my neck. I leaned under Archie's neck as far as I could and fired off a couple shots, just hoping to throw him off balance. As we reached the top of the slope, he leaped at me with a knife in the air, beginning a vicious sweep down at my back. I twisted to grab the knife arm and stopped the blow, but his leap knocked me off the horse. From the corner of my eye, I could see Jim race alongside and pull Anne from the saddle as I went to the ground.

The Apache landed on me as we hit the ground. I was momentarily stunned, but his own momentum carried him over and past, giving me just a moment to recover. I struggled to gain my feet as he turned and came back at me. He looked enormously strong and was clearly very skilled in hand-to-hand fighting. He feigned a move around me, then planted and charged directly at me, knocking me down again. I managed to get one foot under him and shoved him past, but he was back on his feet and on top of me again in an instant. I braced a foot under me and shoved with all my strength, but couldn't push him off me. He swung the knife arm down. I caught his wrist in my hand to momentarily stop the knife. He doubled his other hand into a fist and smashed a couple blows to my face. I thrashed around with my left hand, trying to find a rock or anything I could use as a weapon. There was nothing.

I threw up my left arm to stop another punch aimed at my face, but the knife was moving again. I locked on to his wrist, but felt the strength draining out of me as that knife began an inevitable descent toward my throat. Suddenly, there was a swishing sound and something passed through the air above my head. There was a loud noise as something collided with the Apache's head. He slumped backward and fell away to my left, legs still straddling me. His knife fell to the ground. I shoved him off and grabbed the knife as I struggled to my feet, raising my arm to strike a blow. There was no point. He lay where I had thrown him to the ground, arms and legs twisted at odd angles. There blood on the ground from the head wound.

I spun to my left, knife still in the air, unsure how many more enemies might still be there. I only saw an empty camp, with the remaining Apaches from the camp fleeing into the trees at the northwestern edge of the clearing. I spun again when I registered movement from the corner of my eye. Kate was standing there, holding my father's old Henry rifle. She gripped the barrel in both hands. The gunstock was smashed and splintered.

A wave of relief passed over me. I dropped the knife and pulled in a long, slow breath of air. Kate was staring at the dead warrior on the ground, shock evident on her face. I stepped forward, pulled the Henry from her hands, dropped it on the ground and pulled her in close. She wrapped her arms around my neck and we clung to each other. There were a few gentle sobs as she tried to come to grips with what she'd just done to save my life.

We held on to each other for a few moments, swaying back and forth a little. I remembered a time just over a year ago when she had saved my life with a shot fired from that same Henry rifle. I bent my head and whispered in her ear: "You know, you're downright dangerous when you have that Henry in your hands and I kinda like it." I listened as the sobs gave way to a few chuckles and I knew the shock would soon be replaced by relief.

I looked over Kate's shoulder and saw Anne standing with Jim. Her back was turned to us and her hands were on his shoulders as they talked. Sam was standing by, still holding his rifle as he looked discreetly away. Jim looked over Anne's shoulder and saw Kate and me, both turned now and looking in their direction. We began walking toward them, arms around each other's waists. Jim placed his hands on Anne's waist and gently turned her so she could see us approaching. She watched us silently, not understanding.

"Hello Mother," Kate said. Anne Randolph's knees buckled and she fell to the ground.

Kyle Moore nursed his second beer and glanced again at his pocket watch, occasionally sweeping the saloon with an impatient glance. He shoved the watch back into his pocket and mumbled angrily to himself. Too much time had gone by. They should have been back in town no later than yesterday morning. His anger stemmed mainly from the fact that he didn't know what to do about it. There was far too much money involved for him to give up on this, but where were they? What if they had taken the money to Trinidad or even Denver? It was far too late to track them down and follow them. All he could do was wait here and see if and when they showed up.

He slapped the beer mug down on the table, tossed a few coins after it, and stalked out of the saloon. He stood on the street, looking across at the bank. Part of him wanted to wait outside the bank and watch for them, but that seemed too conspicuous. Besides, there might be too many armed citizens around for him to pull off a robbery here. He knew he needed to go back and wait at the hideout, but he was bored and angry. He stretched, walked up and down the street for a few minutes, then climbed on his horse and rode back out to his hiding spot.

He pulled off the road, walked his horse out of sight and tethered him, then came back to settle down behind the fallen log where he kept watch. He had waited in ambush for a stagecoach or two in times past, but that was nothing compared to the unrelieved boredom of waiting for Reilly and his friends to show up. He leaned back against a tree trunk, pulled his hat down to block the glare from the sun, and stared out at the road. Eventually his eyelids grew heavy and he drifted off to sleep.

A noise from the road penetrated his consciousness and he sat up with a start. A quick look told him it was a solitary man on horseback. Moore sat back against the tree trunk with a snort of frustration. He rose and did some stretches, pacing back and forth. He didn't need to be asleep when the gold passed by.

Eventually he moved a little farther into the trees and began practicing his draw. He worked with both hands, priding himself on his speed. Most men who wore two guns did so just for show or intimidation, but he could draw quickly and shoot accurately with both hands. He had several kills to prove it. The guns leaped into his hands and back to the holsters, first right and then left. He practiced moving a little to his right as he drew. Presenting a moving target was another of his specialties. He told himself that Reilly would stand no chance against him, and he could almost convince himself of it. That little nagging, warning voice in the back of his head only served to anger him. No point thinking about it, anyway. This was going to be a straight ambush for money.

Finally, the lengthening shadows told him it was time he could head back to the hotel. There was no choice but to come back tomorrow and hope this would pay off soon. He rode back into town, stopping off at the saloon before going back to the hotel. Once he finally had the money, he told himself, he would never come back to this miserable little town again.

We took a few minutes to pull ourselves together after rescuing Anne from the Apache camp. She continued to hold on to Jim and Kate, occasionally tracing Kate's face with her fingers as if to convince herself that this was, in fact, her grown daughter. Once in a while she cast an apprehensive glance at the trees where the Apache band had disappeared. Taking our cue from that, the rest of us brought the horses up from the camp we'd set up, preparing to leave. As I placed a foot in the stirrup and prepared to swing up, I felt a hand on my arm. I turned and saw Anne, struggling for words. Finally, she enveloped me in a hug. "Thank you," she said. "That was very brave of you." I looked over her shoulder at Kate, watching us with a look of wonder and joy mixed together. "Seeing the two of you reunited is all the thanks I could ask for," I assured her as I returned the hug.

Retracing our steps of the last two days proved much easier than it had been to find our way here. It also helped that the Apache band we had been dealing with had at least been greatly weakened. So far as we knew, they barely had enough young warriors left to provide food for the rest of the camp. That didn't eliminate the possibility of other bands in the area, so we kept moving rapidly. I noticed that Anne cast frequent glances over her shoulder, as if unable to believe that she was really free and would stay that way. I supposed it would take a fair amount of time for her to adjust.

We reached the encampment where we had rescued Kate just a few days before. Shadows were beginning to lengthen and it was a good time to stop, but we deemed it too unsafe to camp in that same spot. We were running out of food, so I risked a shot to bring down a small buck for food. We moved a few miles further down the trail and pulled off into the trees, using a small fire for cooking before extinguishing it for the night. Anne and Kate spread some blankets on the ground and fell asleep. I was moving to do the same when Jim motioned me over, asking Sam to join us as well.

Jim came right to the point as I sat down on a log beside him. "What route were you planning on taking to get home?" he asked. I shrugged. "The only path I know to take is the one we took to get here. Anything else, I'm risking getting lost out here." Jim nodded, looking absently at the dying embers from the cooking fire. "How much do you trust that guy you let go to not set up an ambush for us?" he asked. "The one with the two tied down guns. Do you think he's above an ambush for all this money?" He nodded toward the gold in the saddle bags. Sam made a sound that sounded a bit like "hmmph" and swung his head around to look at me.

I reflected on the wrathful looks I'd gotten from him, and how he wanted to challenge me to a gunfight in spite of the numbers stacked against him. It didn't seem like a stretch at all to imagine him laying in wait for us to get the gold. I shook my head. "I don't trust him at all," I said. "I just don't know how else to get home." In response, Jim moved over to his saddlebags and fished around in them for a while, emerging finally with a folded, yellowing piece of paper. He moved to the campfire and prodded the embers until he'd produced a small blaze, adequate to shed light on the paper he was holding. I saw that it was a hand-drawn map.

"This is from my days of travelling and trapping a bit during the winter," he told me. "Obviously that's been a few years, because it's from the time before Kate was born. But," he continued, "I think I have a safer route, and I think we can follow it without getting lost because we just have to follow the rivers." I leaned to look over his shoulder while he traced a couple lines on the map with his finger. "This is the Rio Grande River, flowing south, as you see." He moved his finger up and down at the top of the map, indicating the river, which I saw flowed north to south. "The Rio Grande is just west of here," he said. "I'm confident we can reach it by following the game trail we were on when we first left the road to Raton Pass." I nodded. Sam moved a little closer for a look.

"From the Rio Grande," Jim continued, "we cut east over to the Mora River, along about in here." He pointed to another river on the map, this one flowing from west to east. I was more familiar with the Mora River. It ran just a little south of us in Cimarron. I nodded again. "You know when to leave the Rio Grande and cut over to the Mora?" I asked. Jim ran his eyes over the map one more time. "I think I do," he said at length. Sam chipped in. "I used to travel that area myself," he said. "I think it'll work. What's more, I've got a couple fishing lines in my bags and those rivers have some nice trout. We can catch food and stretch our supplies without calling attention to ourselves shooting more deer out here. I like it."

I took one more look at the map and thought again about the would-be robber with the tied-down double guns and angry face. It would be pretty easy to set up an ambush between here and Cimarron, and he'd had plenty of time to do it. "Done deal," I told them. "You guys lead the way and I'm with you. Let's just get home in one piece."

For the first time since we'd left Cimarron, that last stretch went as planned and without complications. The game trail we'd first taken west from the Raton Pass road did indeed take us straight to the Rio

Grande River, which we had no trouble following. Kate and Anne broke out the fishing lines and we dined on some delicious trout the rest of the way home. We cut across as planned, found the Mora River and followed it east until we all recognized familiar landmarks as we neared home. On the third morning after Anne's rescue, we rode into the ranch yard at the Randolph's place, dirty, tired, and happy. Anne's look was priceless as she dismounted, tears running down her face, looking around with wonder. "We're home, Mom," Kate told her. Anne could only nod without words, looking around her at a sight she'd dreamed about for twenty years.

The back door of the ranch house slammed as Mike came across the porch and trotted toward us. His eyes took in Anne Randolph, then he glanced at the bulging saddlebags. He broke into a grin. "Good trip, I take it?" His grin was infectious and the rest of us chuckled and relaxed for the first time in a long time. "Great trip," I said. "Only one thing left before we're done. We need a trip to the bank in Cimarron."

Jim reached out to place a hand on my shoulder. "Anne's been through a lot," he said. "I'd like to stay here and give her a chance to settle in a little before she makes any trips to town." "Of course," I nodded. I looked over at Mike. "You up for giving us a little more security on the trip to town?" Mike turned and headed for the house. "Give me five minutes to saddle up and get my rifle." I turned to Kate. "Your choice," I said. "Stay here or come with us?"

Kate turned and mounted her horse. "I want to see it all the way through," she said. "Besides, I think there are a couple things I can buy in town, now." "You got that right," I told her. Mike returned and we shifted the gold in Jim's saddlebags over to Mike's. Then the four of us turned out through the Randolph gates. After twenty years, George Gibson's gold was finally going to be put to use.

Chapter Eighteen

Bringing It Home

We cantered down the main street in Cimarron, two-by-two. Kate and I were in front, with Sam and Mike following behind us. Sam had the shotgun prominently perched on his right thigh, toothpick waggling in his mouth as he rode. I doubt anybody knew how much gold we had with us, but Sam was an impressive guard, anyway. I glanced backward, and I could tell by the little half-smile on his face that he was thoroughly enjoying this. He didn't know yet that Jim and Kate and I had voted him a one third share in this. That was enough to fix up the saloon and buy him toothpicks for the rest of his life, I reflected. As for me, I was going to need to replenish the herd I'd lost in that flash flood, but that was for another day.

We dismounted and filed into the bank, leaving Mike outside with the shotgun. We didn't need any last-minute surprises with this shipment. We stepped inside, and I was fishing through my mind for the name of the man who had signed over the ranch property to me. Bill... Bill Samuels—the name came to my mind just as he stepped from a back office. He eyed the heavy saddlebags we were all carrying and invited us to step into the back office. We walked past him into the office and thumped the saddlebags down on the desk, one by one. He evaluated the size of the bags and the noise they'd made hitting the desk, then turned back and told the tellers out front he didn't want to be disturbed. He shut the door, sat behind the desk and assured us we had his full attention.

I opened one of the saddlebags and held the top of it open for him. He glanced inside and his jaw dropped a bit. He reached in and extracted a couple of the coins, checking them in the light. "One-dollar gold coins," he mumbled almost to himself. He checked the dates on the coins, mumbling "1849" and "1854" to himself. He pawed through the bag and checked a couple more, then sat down again in his chair. "How many of them are there?" he asked finally. I told him we hadn't counted, but expected the total to be around $5,000. Recovering from his surprise quickly, he pulled out a pad of paper and got down to business. "We'll count it while you're here," he said. He glanced at the three of us. "Is it one third for each of you?" Sam waved his hand and started to say No, but I interrupted. "One third for Jim and Kate, one third each for Sam and me," I told him.

Sam had been lounging back in his chair, feet on the banker's desk. The chair thumped to the floor when his feet came off the desk. He stared at me. "Jim and Kate and I already voted," I told him. "One third for you." He started to speak, cleared his throat, then tried again. It sounded mainly like a croak. "Don't get mushy on me," I told him. "Nobody likes that." He threw his toothpick in my direction and tried again. "I can't tell you what that means to me," he started. His voice faded a little and he tried again. "But I don't want all of it." He waved off my objection. "I could use maybe $500 to fix up some things in the saloon. That's all I want. I have what I need. You have you whole lives in front of you. You take the rest of my share." He stood firm through our objections, and we agreed after a while that's how it would be divided.

Bill Samuels pulled the first saddlebag over, dumped the contents on the desk, and began to count. Kate stood and excused herself. "I've got some things to do," she said. "You tell me how it comes out exactly. She reached toward the pile of coins on the desk. "Can I take twenty of these?" I counted out twenty and started to give them to her. Samuels placed a hand on my arm to stop me, then opened a side drawer on his desk, counted the twenty from a pile of coins in the drawer and gave them to her. He made a note on his pad and Kate left. Then he resumed counting, Sam put his feet back on the desk, and I mostly stared at all that money.

When Samuels was finished counting, we had exactly $5,304. He assured us the money was all good. I think he wanted to ask where it was from, but decided not to ask. He proceeded to divide the money among our accounts. He then asked if we wanted to take any cash with us. Sam declined, but I asked for $50. He did as he had done before, counting the money to me from a side drawer. I accepted the money, asking the obvious question with my expression. He shrugged. "It's probably nothing," he said, "but those coins are all at least twenty-five years old. They're all perfectly legal and spendable, but if you spend a lot of them together, it's possible the wrong people may wonder where they came from and start snooping around. Not at all likely, but I thought I'd spare you any possible questions. I replaced them with dollar coins issued just last year. "If," he continued, "you need to withdraw quite a bit at once, like maybe $100 or more, just give me a couple days' notice to make sure I have enough cash on hand."

Those were things that wouldn't have occurred to me. We each thanked him and left the bank, stopping to compare notes on the porch. Sam was anxious to get back to the saloon and see how things were going. Mike accompanied him down to the saloon, with the understanding he would be back at the ranch within a couple hours to fill me in on anything that had happened while we were gone.

Kyle Moore was in a foul mood as he paid his bill at the hotel desk. An additional five days had gone by, five of the most crushingly boring days of his life. He had hung out at his ambush spot each day. He conceded that he hadn't managed to stay awake all day every day, but mostly he had. He was quite sure that Reilly and his party had not come through. He could only conclude now that they had taken the money somewhere else. He slapped a few coins on the desk, picked up his rifle and bags, then went outside to strap them down on his horse.

He strapped his rifle into the scabbard, glancing over his saddle and down the main street as he did so. He finished with the rifle, reached down to adjust his gun belt, and turned to step into the saddle. He turned and looked back down the street in disbelief. Reilly, the old saloonkeeper, the girl, and one of the fresh-faced kids from the saloon had just dismounted in front of the bank. They lifted saddlebags from their horses and carried them up the steps into the bank. The kid from the saloon settled down on the porch with a shotgun. Moore felt the blood rushing to his face as he slapped the horse in anger. He knew full well what was in those saddlebags and he had missed his chance. They'd come from the other direction.

Moore stayed where he was, red-faced, kicking at the dirt, until he gradually became aware of the stares coming from passers-by. With effort, he stepped back, calmed himself, and walked slowly across the street. He entered the town café, where he had eaten entirely too many meals now, asked for coffee at a table near the window. He wanted to watch the street unobserved. He tilted his face down toward the table when anyone passed by, aware that he was usually red-faced when he was as angry as he was now. He looked up once in a while to size up the situation across the street.

After several minutes the girl came out by herself and turned toward the general store. He watched her enter the store then turned his attention back to the bank. Reilly and the old saloonkeeper were still inside. And, of course, there was the kid on the porch with the shotgun. The rage inside him began to ebb as he considered what he could do now. The possibility of ambush was obviously gone. The money was in the bank. That didn't necessarily mean he couldn't get to it. He thought again about the two idiot partners he'd left behind. The fool who went against Reilly and all those backup guns and didn't live to tell about it. And the coward who had gone up to Trinidad and Dodge City. He could have used either one of them now. Still, he reasoned, this was an easy town. No sheriff to worry about.

He stirred his coffee as the basics of a plan began to form in his mind. It revolved around the question of whether or not he could take down the bank by himself. He'd been in there—just a couple tellers and a bank manager. He could handle them, assuming he could get his hands on the money before a crowd had a chance to form outside the door. That left the townspeople. Would anybody here stand in his way? Chance Reilly. The name leaped into his mind immediately. He could wait until Reilly left town, but he wanted to take the man down in public. It would send a message and nobody would stand up to him if he'd taken Reilly down. The old saloonkeeper with the shotgun, maybe. He would have to deal with him too, but he could deal with them one at a time. Reilly first.

Moore left the café, glancing only briefly across at the bank as he continued on down to where he had left his horse tethered. He felt the excitement rise in him as he pictured things going down. He would call out Reilly in the street. After he'd killed Reilly, he would ride out of town and give it a couple hours to let things settle down just a bit. They would clear the street and go back to their shops and businesses. Then he would come back for the bank. He looked back down the street. The girl had come out of the general store, carrying a package. She tied it down on her horse, then started across the street toward the café. As she reached the sidewalk on the other side, Reilly and the old man came out of the bank and hesitated on the boardwalk in front. Then the old man headed toward the saloon with the kid and Reilly turned toward the general store. Moore cursed under his breath. He would have to wait and challenge Reilly after he came out of the general store.

Kate left the bank and turned toward the general store, enjoying the weight of the twenty dollars in her pocket. Having money free to spend was a bit of a rarity for her, although she had saved up these twenty dollars over the last year. She hadn't had time to withdraw it before this morning, but she had it now and she hoped her order had come in at the general store. She suspected Chance might come this way after leaving the bank, and she wanted to be in and out before he got there.

She stepped into the general store, enjoying the scents of some candles lighted in the store window. The owner, Dave Purvis came forward to meet her. She was too interested in what she'd come for to spend any time on small talk. "Hi Dave," she said, "has it arrived yet?" Purvis chuckled at her directness, but nodded his head. "Yeah, it came the day before yesterday, Kate," he said. "Would you like to try it on?" Kate's eyes lit up. "Yes, but I need to do it fast." She followed him to the back of the store, where he lifted a long white dress from a package. "As ordered," he told her. "Your wedding dress." Kate held it up in front of her, looking in the mirror, then whirled around. "Where can I change?" Purvis pointed to his office, and Kate dashed in that direction. "Kate," he said, "am I being nosy if I ask if you're absolutely sure you're going to have a need for that dress?" "Yes," she called back as she closed the door, "you are being nosy and I AM sure I'm going to need this dress." The door clicked shut.

Purvis thought back to his own wedding and chuckled. His wife had, in fact, had a much better idea of what was going to happen than he did. Kate probably did know she'd need that dress. He chuckled again and moved to the front of the store to wait on another customer. He expected Chance to show up this morning also, but Kate didn't know that yet. That brought another smile to his face. After another five minutes or so, Kate came back with the dress and asked him to wrap it up. "Everything good?" he asked. "Perfect!" said Kate. She paid and hurried out the door with her package.

Kate walked over to where she had left her horse, tethered to the rail outside the bank. There was no sign of Chance or Sam yet, and Mike confirmed they were still inside the bank. She tucked the package into her bags, still on the saddle from the trip. She pulled a blanket over the package and crossed the street to the café. She ordered a coffee and waited for Sam and Chance to finish their business at the bank. She noticed a man sitting on the bench, just down the street. He looked a little familiar, but his hat was pulled low over his face and she couldn't quite recognize him.

I left the bank with fifty gold dollars in my pockets and another $2,402 in the bank. We had taken the banker into our confidence about the source of the money. Samuels felt that with more than twenty years gone by and nobody stepping forward to offer a reward or mount a trip to recover the money, we could safely consider it ours. He had made a point of telling us he would tell no one about where the money came from. "Lost treasures have a way of attracting bad folks," was what he'd said to us.

I looked around briefly for Kate, but didn't see her on Main Street. I figured she was probably in a shop somewhere. I hoped she wouldn't be in the general store. My business there would have to wait if I found her there. I turned and walked the half block to the general store, hearing a little bell go off when I stepped inside. Dave Purvis came forward to meet me. I shook his hand while glancing quickly around to see if Kate was there. Dave smiled and told me Kate had left a few minutes ago. He seemed to think that was pretty funny. I looked at him suspiciously, wondering if he knew something I didn't but the smile disappeared from his face and he took me to the back.

He took me to his office at the rear of the store, produced some keys from his pocket, unlocked a drawer and set a small black box on the desk. "There it is, just what you ordered," he told me. "Gold wedding ring. That's for Kate, right?" The same small smile appeared around the edges of his mouth. "Right," I said, staring at him suspiciously again. "Who else?" "Of course," he mumbled around the grin. Then the smile disappeared again.

I opened the box and took the ring out, examining it in the light. I didn't know much about wedding rings, but it certainly looked like the one in Dave's catalogue and I thought Kate would like it. After a couple minutes I put it back in the box and pulled all the gold coins out of my pocket, setting them down on the desk. "How much was it?" I asked, knowing the answer. "Twenty dollars," came the answer. OK, I thought, he's not going to give me a bargain. I began to separate the necessary number of coins on the desk.

Dave looked at the pile of coins on the desk and watched me separate them for a few seconds. Then he reached back into the drawer, pulled out another box and opened it. "I went ahead and ordered a couple more with yours," he told me. "I'm sure I'll have another customer or two for this sort of thing. Take a look at this one. It's a wider, heavier gold band and even has a couple little diamonds in it. See?" I remained rooted where I was, looking at the ring without touching it. "How much is that one?" I asked. "Forty dollars" came the answer. I moaned inwardly, but reached out and took the box, admiring the sparkle I could see with just the light from the window filtering through. I tilted it back and forth a few times. "OK," I said resignedly, "I'll take this one."

Dave reached out and expertly pushed ten of the coins back to me, dropping the others in a cash box that appeared from under the desk. I put my ten coins back in my pockets and noticed how much lighter those pockets felt. No wonder the man ran a store. He could make money on a deserted island. I took the ring box, put it in my other pocket, and turned to go. He stopped me at the doorway, looking serious now.

"I know we've talked about it before, but I'm speaking for the whole town as mayor," he began. I stopped him. "It's not about being sheriff, is it?" He nodded. "This town is growing, and there's more money coming in every day to the stores and the bank." He looked over at the cash box under the desk. "It looks like you just brought some more in, yourself. Folks need to feel safe." I held up my hand to forestall anything more on the subject. "It's just not for me, Dave. If you need to deputize some people for something, you can call on me to be one of them. That's about it. I'm not a lawman and I don't know how to be one. You're going to need someone else." He acknowledged what I'd said with an unhappy nod, shook my hand and saw me out the door. I stepped out to the porch, looking for Kate again.

Chapter Nineteen

Confrontation

Anne Randolph lay on the bed in Kate's room, tossing and turning uncomfortably. She had sat with Jim on the porch for quite some time after the others had left. Mainly Jim had caught her up on things at the ranch and the life he and Kate were living there. He had made no effort to press her for any details of her life in captivity, nor any plans she might have for the future. She was very grateful to him for that. He had made it clear she was welcome to stay. She tossed on the bed a couple more times, trying to absorb what had happened in the last two days. The change in her life was going to be enormous. She had long ago accepted that she would live out her life as an Apache, and the change was almost too much to process right now.

Another toss on the bed and she realized she simply wouldn't be able to fall asleep there. She got up and looked around Kate's room curiously. Mostly there were flowers and a few mementos that meant nothing to Anne. She opened the door to the room and looked out. Jim had gone to check on the cattle, probably mainly to give her some privacy and time alone. She went out to the kitchen and looked around, eventually remembering how she'd made coffee in this same kitchen so long ago. She took her cup out to the porch and sat down, looking out at the ranch yard. The bunkhouse had been built since she had left. Everything else looked familiar.

The fact that their daughter was now a grown young woman was the most impactful thing of all. In her mind, she knew that much time had gone by, but she'd only been able to picture Kate as a small girl up until now. And apparently, she had a future planned with the boy who'd been their neighbor. What had his dad called him? "Boy-o" she repeated to herself, smiling softly. Boy-o had grown up to be a young man named Chance, one who had risked his life for her. Actually, she knew now he had risked it for Kate, which certainly made her no less grateful. She remembered how Kate and Chance had looked together, and the look Kate wore when he was around. It brought another smile to Anne's face, this one lasting quite a while.

She came back mentally to her current situation. Could she even fit in here now? Just being indoors felt cramped and uncomfortable.

Could she be accepted in a small town like Cimarron after she had lived in the wild for twenty years? What would anybody think about the way she had run away? Could her family even really accept her after that? The questions were too much to answer at the present. She stood up and paced back and forth on the porch.

She came back to anchoring herself on the things she knew. The biggest mistake in her life had been the result of a sudden, impetuous decision. She had resolved long ago not to make her decisions that way again. The moment when Chance had pulled her up on his horse and out of the camp was an obvious exception. She'd had only a second to decide, and she was happy with that decision. Her future was a different matter, and she knew this much for a fact: she would take her time and make a careful choice this time around. She finished the coffee, spread a blanket on the porch and laid down. She was asleep almost instantly.

Moore leaned up against a post in front of the barber shop, trying to remain as calm as possible. He grabbed a stick and started whittling, trying to appear nonchalant. He didn't need a local town dweller guessing his intentions and getting in the way. He glanced again at the general store. Reilly had been in there for a while. Still no sign of him coming out. He gave up his pretense at whittling after just a few strokes and returned the knife to his belt.

He concentrated on the street in front of him, picturing how it would go down. Reilly's horse was tethered behind where Moore now stood and across the street, in front of the bank. That meant

Reilly would very likely be coming in this direction to get his horse. He glanced behind him to make sure the saloonkeeper and the kid were still gone. There was no one in front of the bank now. He looked back up the street, mentally measuring how much distance he wanted between them when they drew. He figured he could step directly into the middle of the street, then call him out.

He didn't really worry about anybody else getting involved once they'd squared off. This would be a man-to-man fight and people would stay out of it. Besides, once he'd taken down Reilly they would be scared of him. That would come in handy when he came back this afternoon to rob the bank. He shielded his eyes with his hat and his hand and looked up at the sun. It was mid-morning, so the sun was only half up, behind him and to his right a bit. He would move in that direction when he drew, putting the sun in Reilly's eyes.

It seemed he had been there for an eternity. He began to worry that Reilly might have seen him through a store window and left through a back door. He noticed idly that Reilly's girl was now in the café at the same table he'd been at. She seemed to be watching for him to leave the store also. Moore glanced behind him a couple times to reassure himself that Reilly hadn't slipped out to approach him from the rear. He was beginning to move to a different spot when at last the door to the general store opened and Reilly stepped out.

Moore touched both guns to reassure himself they were there and ready for use. He took five steps to the middle of the street and squared himself around as Reilly stepped off the porch. "Reilly," he called out. "I've come to take you down."

Kate lingered over her coffee in the café, wondering what was taking Chance so long in there. Normally he could pick up whatever he wanted and be out of there, but now he'd been in there for a good fifteen minutes. Did the general store carry jewelry? Now there was a thought to put a smile on her face.

Her thoughts turned to how things would be at home after her mother's return. Kate had taken it for granted that she would stay with them this time and her parents would be back together. She realized now it wasn't a certainty. It would take time. She resolved to be patient and knew that Jim would be also. There was no telling what her mother had been through in the last twenty years.

A movement in the street attracted her attention. She looked out to see the man she'd seen on the bench across the street earlier. His profile still looked familiar, but his hat was pulled low over his face and she couldn't get a good look at him. He stopped in the middle of the street. Her eyes dropped and for the first time she noticed that he wore double tied-down guns around his waist. His head came up as he glanced briefly her way, and she gasped in alarm. She jumped from her chair to get outside, then she knew it was too late. Chance was stepping out from the general store. The bandit from the caves was squared off to face him, hands down near his gun belt.

I had stepped off the boardwalk and down to the street when I heard my name called. I looked up, squinting just a bit into the morning sun. For just a moment I thought it was Mike, my employee, but the voice wasn't quite recognizable. Then I saw one of the three menen who had tried to hold us up at the cave where we found the gold. It was the one who seemed to fancy himself a gunfighter—the one with two tied-down guns. I moved a bit toward the center of the street so I wouldn't be staring directly into the sun. I stopped and looked at him. The situation was all too familiar. I'd had a gun battle with a man named Yates Carson in this same street a little over a year ago. This man in front of me seemed equally determined to draw on me.

"What seems to be the problem?" I asked. He didn't seem to be expecting to talk to me, and it seemed to throw him off stride a little. A few people had stopped in front of the shops. He glanced over at them, licked his lips nervously and shouted, "You murdered my partner!" I stared at him. "What's your name?" I asked. That one threw him again. He stared at me and regrouped enough to say, "Kyle Moore." "Well Kyle, he drew on me while the three of you were trying to rob me and my friends. Can you really call that murder?"

It was another question designed to make him stop and rethink a few things. He hesitated, hands hovering around his gun belt, trying to regroup. He'd come to shoot me and move on. He hadn't expected to be having a conversation. I could see in his eyes there was a moment of indecision. I kept my eyes locked on his and paused to see if he would back down and walk away. I noticed he seemed off balance, leaning slightly to his right. He glanced at the gathering crowd, then looked back in my direction, not really focused. I could see confusion, fear and anger in his eyes, all at once.

His eyes dropped to the ground, a picture of indecision. Then his head snapped up and his eyes came up to my chest, hand sweeping down for his gun. I drew and fired, but he had lunged to his right even as he fired. I felt a burning sensation across my left shoulder and my shot missed, blasting through the space he had just vacated. His shot had been thrown off by his movement, just grazing my shoulder and I tracked him with my gun, knowing he would have to steady down to get off a good shot. There! His right foot planted and he began to square up. I fired again, driving a shot through the center of his chest. He was blown backwards to his knees, gun flying out of his hand. I held the gun steady on the middle of his chest, waiting. Somehow, he remained on his knees and his left hand clawed the second gun out of the holster, his face a mask of rage and hatred. I shifted my aim a few inches to the right and fired again. He pitched over backwards, left gun spilling into the dirt. His head hit the ground and bounced before coming to rest.

I stared dully down the street at the sight of another dead man lying in front of me. I felt the shock and a touch of nausea strike me as I holstered my gun. I looked over as Doc Chapman came hurrying from his office, moving people back from the body. He set his bag down and bent over the body in the street. I turned away again, looking for a place to sit down, knowing what Doc Chapman would say. The third bullet had gone directly through his heart.

"Chance!" Her voice came to me through the babble of voices I heard in the street, cutting through the noise surrounding the body of Kyle Moore. I stopped and looked for her. She was running from the café; I could see her now, running toward me. She enveloped me in a quick hug, then took her hands away and looked at them, seeing the red on one hand. "You're bleeding!" I remembered now the burning feeling on my left shoulder, glancing down at it as I turned toward her. "It's nothing," I assured her. "A scratch." "We'll let Doc Chapman decide that," she told me. She ran over to pull him through the crowd as he rose after examining the corpse. He set his bag down beside me and ripped the shirt sleeve away from my shoulder.

We're going to sew that one up," he announced after looking at the shoulder. He led me away to his office, Kate following. He sat me down in a chair and pulled a bottle from the bag. "This will hurt a little," he advised me, then poured some liquid on the wound. I gritted my teeth while Kate grabbed my hand. He pulled something like thread out of his bag along with a needle. "This is catgut," he told me. "This will hurt a little more." "Doc, you're a lot of fun," I told him. He passed me a folded towel. "Bite down on this," he said. "If nothing else it will keep you quiet."

After about fifteen minutes of Doc's tender mercies we were finally done. I hoped I wouldn't need to see him again anytime soon. He told me not to do any heavy lifting for a couple weeks and left for a call out of town. Kate announced she was going to get me some whiskey. I thought that was the best idea I'd heard all day. I eased back in the chair, looking at the sling on my shoulder. I decided that if this was the worst thing to happen after all the events of the last several days, I was probably pretty lucky.

The front door to the office opened and closed. Kate came in, giving a kiss and the whiskey, in that order. She squeezed in next to me on the chair. Sam appeared in the doorway, holding his shotgun. Mike followed him in, carrying a rifle and wearing a side gun on his hip. I looked at the weapons, then at Sam. "There was another one of them," he reminded me. "There were three of them at the holdup." I thought back to the robbery attempt at the caves. That seemed like a month ago, but I nodded, remembering the one who had laid down his weapons first. Sam glanced over at Mike, then back at me. "We've searched the town from end to end and asked quite a few people if they've seen somebody that looks like him. We don't think he's here, but we're going to keep an eye out. Now go home and get well." He rested a hand briefly on my good shoulder and Mike nodded at me. I watched them leave, counting myself lucky to have these men as friends.

Kate reached down to hold the hand on my good arm and rested her head on my shoulder. "We need to have a quieter life," she said at length. "We don't need any more of this. I don't know what I would do if I lost you now." I glanced down at the outline of the ring box in my pocket. "We're going to have a good life together," I assured her. "Let's go home."

We left the doctor's office, reaching the street just as Mayor Purvis came out of his store. The barber doubled as the undertaker in Cimarron, and I could see his helpers carrying the body away. The crowd was dispersing slowly as people drifted back to the stores they'd come from. Purvis walked up to us, watching as the street starting to come back to normal. "You OK?" he asked. I nodded. He glanced at me, cleared his throat and looked away, debating about what he wanted to say. "We're lucky you were here to deal with him," he began. "He might have come here to rob the bank." I shook my head, "No, he just had a personal grudge with me," I told him. We started to move away but he stopped us. "Chance we could use you…" he began. "No," I cut him off. "Not for me, Dave. You can find a sheriff somewhere else." He nodded in resignation and turned to go back to his general store. We moved on to the horses.

Kate mounted and waited while I figured out how to mount with one good arm. "You didn't tell me he wanted you for sheriff," she said. I walked around to mount from the other side, struggled aboard Archie and looked over at her. "That was just before I left on the cattle drive," I said. "There was so much going on. I guess I forgot. Anyway, I said no. Actually, I guess I've said no a couple times now." We moved the horses out to the street and walked them slowly out of town. "We'll go to our house," she told me. "I'm going to keep an eye on you for a while. You can rest on the couch for the rest of the day." I shook my head. "My house first," I told her. "Just for a short while. Then we can go to your house." She looked puzzled but nodded her agreement. I checked my pocket with my good hand to be sure the ring was still there.

We rode slowly out to the ranch, then turned in at my gate and rode up to the house. It seemed to me that our favorite place had been on the porch of this house, resting after working on our future home together and looking out at the meadow running down to those juniper trees. I led her up to the porch. She started to sit down in the chairs we'd put on the porch, but I took both her hands and turned to her.

I'd rehearsed what I wanted to say, but all of a sudden, my tongue didn't seem to be up to the job. I started and stopped a couple times, and I could see the comprehension growing in her eyes. She waited for me to get it together. "Kate," I finally said. "In many ways I feel like my life just started when I met you and I don't ever want to be without you. I just know this is our forever, right here in this place. Will you marry me?" I watched as a growing smile lit that beautiful face. "Yes," she said simply. "I'll marry you."

Made in the USA
Columbia, SC
01 September 2019